THE PROMISE OF HADES

THE HADES TRIALS

ELIZA RAINE

ROSE WILSON

Editors: Christopher Mitchell, Kyra Wilson

Cover: Kim's Covers

*For everyone who is convinced that
there's a goddess of hell inside them...*

ONE

PERSEPHONE

'Wait, wait, wait. Slow down. You seriously expect me to believe that you were kidnapped by Zeus and taken to *Olympus*?' My brother stared at me as I paced frantically up and down my small room, his hazel eyes wide.

'Yes! It's true. I was there for weeks.'

'Persy, I spoke to you on the phone yesterday.' He ran a hand through his sandy hair and shook his head as he glanced around my trashed room. 'Should I call mom? Are you OK?'

I stopped pacing and screwed my face up. Gods, I'd love to see my mom and dad. But they were nearly a thousand miles away in their RV, touring Atlanta. And if Sam phoned them and told them I was babbling about being kidnapped, they would likely use the little money they had to fly back to New York. The selfish part of me wanted nothing more, but the rational part of me answered Sam.

'No,' I sighed, and sat down. 'Don't call them.'

'Tell me again what happened,' he said, his voice gentle. 'And... What are you wearing and why is your hair white?'

I had called my brother the second my wracking sobs and blind rage had lessened enough for me speak. If I had any question or doubt about the strength of my feelings for Hades, the shock of him leaving me had completely dispelled them.

It felt like a piece of my chest was missing; breathing, thinking, walking - *everything* was now staggered and difficult. The sense of wrongness I felt when I looked around my room only served to widen the gaping hole inside me.

I'd never felt betrayal and rejection like it. I *couldn't* have left him like that. I couldn't have flashed myself away, knowing I would never see him again. My body and mind wouldn't have let me do it, I was sure.

Which I knew was irrational. Not a day earlier I had told him I didn't even know if I wanted to be with him. But the moment I had heard him say those words, *a light this bright can't be kept in the dark,* something gripped my insides in a vice-like hold. Something bright and hot and intensely fierce. It carried his sadness, his passion, his love, straight into my heart and it had over-whelmed me. And it had flared to life only long enough to be doused out seconds later, when he'd flashed from the room, leaving me for good.

. . .

I'd cried so hard I'd almost thrown up. Then anger took over, fury forcing the tears out. Before I knew what I was doing I was launching my belongings around my room, cushions and clothes flying. Then I had noticed my purse on the bed, along with my leather biker jacket, and sense had bled through my rage. I'd dug out my cell phone and plugged it in to charge, then called Sam.

He was at my door faster than I thought possible, and I'd thrown myself at him, fresh tears filling my eyes as I took in his concerned face. A face I never thought I would see again. When I was done sobbing and hugging him, I had tried to tell him what had happened. Unsuccessfully, it seemed.

'I'm not from America. I'm from a place called Olympus, which is ruled by the Greek gods. I was married to Hades before, but I did something awful and they sent me here to have a new life as a human mortal, with no memories.' Sam stared at me, eyebrows high, and I took a deep breath. Was what I was saying even possible?

There was no way I could have imagined it all. Hades' silver eyes filled my mind. No way whatsoever. They were real.

'And Zeus kidnapped you?' my brother prompted.

'Yes. Hades disobeyed him publicly and created a new realm in Olympus, so to punish him Zeus let a bunch of women compete to be his wife, and he took me from New York to force me to compete too.'

Real concern was now clear on Sam's face.

'You were competing to marry Hades? The devil?'

'Yes. I'm wearing this torn, burnt dress because I was in the middle of a Trial that went wrong. I ended up in Tartarus.'

Sam stood up.

'We need to go to the emergency room. You've had a stroke or something,' he said, his voice strained.

'And you think having a stroke extended to dying my hair white and doing this to a ballgown?' I asked, waving my shredded skirt at him. 'I'm serious Sam, I'm telling the truth.'

'But, Persy, that's not possible. It's simply not possible.'

'That's what I thought at first, but it is! I had power, Sam!'

'Power?'

'Yes, I could make plants grow. And I had vines that came out of my palms!'

'Like fucking Spiderman? Persy, we need to go to the emergency room. Now.'

'No,' I said, shaking my head.

'Then what the hell do you want me to do?' He threw his hands in the air and glared at me.

'I need to get back there,' I whispered. Sam's mouth fell open.

'To the place where you were competing to marry the devil?' I nodded. 'You want to go back there?'

Something that might have been relief washed through me as I answered Sam's question.

'Yes.' I *did* want to go back. To Hades. I had to be where he was. I finally had one solid decision made in my head. Dread replaced my relief fast though. I was no longer trapped in the Underworld. Now I was trapped in New York.

I had no way of getting to Hades.

'I gotta call mom, Persy. This is fucked up, you're not well.' Sam moved to my side slowly, putting an arm around me as he sat down. I lifted my hand and peered at my palm, digging deep inside myself to feel for my power.

There was nothing.

'Sam, I've never fit in. Now I know why,' I whispered.

'Maybe you've invented being married to the devil to try to make yourself feel stronger?' he said gently. 'Perhaps you've been under too much pressure with the program at the botanical gardens or...' He trailed off, his face darkening. 'Did something bad happen? Has someone hurt you?'

'No! I swear to you, nothing awful has happened to me and triggered some sort of mental breakdown,' I told him firmly, and his face relaxed. 'But Sam, I *am* stronger. I was a freaking goddess. All this time.'

I felt a flare of something deep in my stomach, a stab of rage and pain, and I gasped as I realized it wasn't coming from me. *It was Hades.* I could sense his dark smoky power under the physical feeling. It was the same as what I'd felt before he had left, though the emotion wasn't sadness now. It was primal and animalistic, filled with fear and fury.

He was breaking. I could feel it.

'The bond,' I murmured, my skin crawling as the feeling spread through me. 'I have to help him,' I said, looking up at Sam, the urgency I felt making my voice crack. 'He made a mistake leaving me here, I have to help him.'

'Help who?'

'Hades. He's in trouble.'

'Erm, I'm sure the Lord of the Dead can handle himself,' Sam said, more calmly than his face suggested he was.

'No. No, I have to get back.' I leaped to my feet, yet more tears burning the back of my eyes. Pain and rage spasmed through me, and I almost cried out. Sam stood up fast, taking my wrist in his hand.

'Come on. We'll get help.'

I started to go with him, toward the door, but faltered as I realized what he meant.

'I'm not ill, Sam, I swear!' Frustration was welling inside me, my own anger mingling with the intense fury flowing into me from the bond to Hades.

My brother's grip on my wrist tightened, even as his face softened.

'I'm sorry, Persy, but we need to get you help.' He tugged me and I stumbled. He would never hurt me, but if he thought he was helping me I wouldn't be surprised if he picked me up and slung me over his shoulder. He was a lot bigger than I was.

'Sam, stop!'

My shout was cut off though, as blinding white light filled the room.

Sam let go of me as we both threw our arms in front of our eyes instinctively. Hope surged through me. Was it Hades? *Please, please let it be Hades.* I blinked furiously, and let out a cry of relief as a figure came into focus in front of me.

'Hecate!' I half sobbed, and threw myself at her. If it wasn't Hades, Hecate was the next best thing. She could take me to him.

'Erm, I don't do hugs,' she said, patting me awkwardly on the back as I wrapped my arms around her.

'P-Persy?' I heard Sam's almost whispered voice behind me, and let go of Hecate to turn to him. 'Persy, who is your outrageously hot friend and how did she appear out of thin air?' His face was pale, his hazel eyes huge.

'Outrageously hot, huh? I like him,' Hecate said, looking at me. 'He can come too, if you like.'

'I need to get to Hades, something awful is happening,' I said to her, ignoring my brother and gripping her shoulder urgently.

'Why the fuck do you think I'm here? Much as I like you, Persy, I wouldn't risk crossing every freaking god in Olympus if I didn't have a damned good reason.' Her face was serious, her eyes sparking with blue power. 'He's snapped, Persy. I've never seen wrath like it. So far we've been able to keep him in the Underworld, but he's too strong. If he gets out or Zeus discovers that he has lost control like this and put all of Olympus in danger...' She trailed off, her meaning clear. Ice seemed to snake down my spine, my skin fizzing with fear.

'Zeus would kill him?'

'Or worse.'

'Take me to him. Now,' I said.

In answer, the world flashed white.

TWO

PERSEPHONE

I f it weren't for the fiercely strong grip Hades had over my emotions, I would have begged Hecate to take me back to New York the second my eyes cleared.

We were standing in a cavern similar to the Empusa's lair, except it was much bigger, the walls glowing deep red and the smell almost unbearable.

There were bodies everywhere. Few of them appeared to be human, but all of them looked as though they had been ripped apart by an animal. Trying desperately to ignore my roiling stomach, I scanned the gruesome space for Hades but saw only corpses.

'Shit, he's moved,' muttered Hecate, then I heard heaving and retching. I turned, and felt the blood drain from my face as I saw my brother, spewing his guts up onto the cavern floor.

'Sam? Hecate, why the fuck did you bring him here?'

'I told you he could come with us, now shut up,' she said, and her eyes turned white as she glowed blue. 'Shit, shit, shit, he's nearly at the mouth of Tartarus,' she said, and grabbed and me and Sam, before flashing again.

The river of fire we'd been transported to flared into life beside us, but I didn't even notice it.

Hades was *monstrous*.

There was no other word for him. He was the size of a building as he moved towards the cave mouth, his back to us. His body seemed swollen with hulking muscle, and something black was moving under his skin, licks of smoke coiling from him. Blue light emanated from his body, but there was no army of defensive corpses forming around him this time. The light was forming a carpet of carnage in his wake, broken bodies with faces twisted in terror surrounding him as he screamed.

'Campe! I'm coming for you!'

I heard a thump behind me, and spun to see Sam collapsed on the ground.

'Hecate, get him out of here, he's human, he'll die!' As I said the words I felt my vines spring to life in my palms.

Without a word Hecate knelt to grab my brother, and they disappeared.

'You're next, Cronos!' bellowed Hades.

'Hades!' I yelled, as loudly as I could. He didn't falter, only a foot from the cave mouth now. 'Hades!' I tried again, and launched my vines at him. Just as his foot moved into the darkness, my black vines wrapped around his enormous shoulders.

Darkness consumed me completely.

Kill. Die. Fear. Burn. Blood.

The words hammered through my head and I gasped, dropping to one knee. There was no light. Only sparks of life flaring in my vision, calling to me. They needed to be extinguished. Everything needed to die. Fear always won. It could not be conquered. Death was the only certainty.

'Persephone?' The voice was strained, but light crept back into the edges of my vision as the sound of my name filtered through to me. 'Persephone, is that really you?'

'Yes,' I gritted out, unable to see him, but sure it was Hades speaking. 'You have to stop.'

'I can't. I can't.'

'Please. I feel it now. The bond. Can't you?' Hot tears streamed down my cheeks as wave after wave of hatred and violence crashed down the vines, flowing into me, poisoning me.

Kill. Kill them all. Tear them apart. Leave nothing. None of them deserve to live.

'The monster inside me is too strong. It will always win.' Hades' voice was suddenly hard and cold, and the little light seeped away again fast.

'No! You can fight it, you're not a monster!' I shouted, but the torrent of fury coming from him said differently. He was *worse* than a monster. He didn't just want to destroy, he wanted to torture. To ruin, to break, to brutalize.

I had to sever the connection to him, I had to remove my vines. I couldn't take his power, couldn't handle the fearsomely brutal desires. He had told me that he was too strong for me to ever steal his power, and he had been right. There was too much, it could flow endlessly into me and he would still be just as strong. It felt like he was filling me with his wrath, and every second I held on I lost more of myself. Why did my power do this? Why couldn't I take the fury away from him, instead of turning myself into something just as awful?

The gold vines. The thought powered through the cascade of furious darkness. *The gold vines did the opposite of the black ones.*

I willed the vines that I could no longer see to turn from black to gold, clinging desperately to the remnants of my infatuation with him, the strength of my connection to him, the desire to make him happy, content, loved. I recalled everything Hecate had told me about him, how he'd given up parts of himself to serve Olympus, how he had been forced to become this beast by his brother. I filled my head with the feeling of his lips on mine, his hands on my skin, his beautiful silver eyes, always so filled with emotion when he looked at me. He had created life. As much of him that craved death and destruction wanted life and light. I could give that to him.

I poured my power into my vines, praying it was reaching him.

'Persephone.'

I opened my eyes and gasped, shocked by the light. I focused on Hades, and took in a deep breath. He was still huge, but the blue glow and all the bodies had gone. The new light was coming from the gold vines stretching from me to him, morphing into shining tattoos that coiled around his shoulders and chest, covering almost all of his skin.

His eyes were fixed on mine, silver and stunning and haunted.

'Hades,' I breathed. 'You're back.'

'So are you,' he croaked, and thudded to his knees.

THREE

HADES

S*he was back.*

I was vaguely aware of Hecate, and her flashing us somewhere else, but I didn't let go of Persephone's hand, didn't take my eyes from her tear-filled green ones.

She was back.

'I'm sorry,' I said, as she pushed me backward. I felt my legs hit something and sat down hard. My head was still full of darkness, but it was receding. The beast called to me, but green and gold light burned hot through my body, drowning out its voice, piecing my barriers back together, reinforcing them with glowing vines. Her power.

'Sorry for what? Dumping me in New York, or nearly getting yourself killed?' she snapped, and I blinked. She shoved something into my hands. 'Drink. Now.'

I did as I was bid, the sweet taste of nectar forcing the evil thoughts even further into the recesses. I realized I was still twice her size as I drained the tiny glass too quickly, and shrank myself down.

'I'll leave you to it, boss,' Hecate said, but I still didn't look at her. I couldn't take my eyes from Persephone. My Queen. My savior.

'Thanks, Hecate. And, erm, please be nice to Sam,' Persephone said to her.

'As if I'd be anything else,' Hecate responded, and there was a flash. Persephone looked back at me, and her face was stern. 'I'm only here because Hecate cares so much about you. You're an idiot,' she said, exasperation and fear mingling on her beautiful face. 'If Zeus found out that you lost control like that, what would he do?'

'He would give my job to someone else, and leave me in Tartarus for eternity,' I answered. And that's what I had wanted. There was no life without her. No point existing. And I was a monster. I was destined for that hell-hole in the end anyway.

'Hades, you are bound to me, and I to you. Even in New York, I could feel your suffering. Do you think it was fair to put me through that?' Her voice was strained, and I realized she was barely containing her emotion.

Electricity seemed to spark through my body as she

spoke, and something the monster had snuffed out completely leaped back to life. *Hope.*

'You feel the bond?'

'Yes. I feel it. I feel you. And you were right. It's not something. It's *everything.*' I reached for her, but she stepped backward, out of my grasp. 'Hades, you need to understand. I felt what is inside you. And it is evil and cruel and toxic.' Her voice shook as she spoke, and I could feel the devastation closing in around me. The monster was stronger than the bond. *The monster was stronger than everything.* 'Instead of fighting it, instead of letting me help you, you left me. You left me and you let it win.'

She wasn't mad at the monster, I realized. *She was mad at me.* Shame washed over me as her expression hardened.

'You are the King of the Underworld. If I am to be your Queen one day, you need to start fucking acting like one.' My mouth dropped open. 'Everything here bows to you, the worst and most vicious demons, the cruelest gods trapped in Tartarus, all of it. That thing inside you is no stronger than they are.' I stared at her. She was right. Why had I never seen it that way? 'And if the one thing that would allow you to lose control of it is losing the woman you're bonded to, why the fuck would you do something as stupid as leaving me?'

'I... I had no choice,' I whispered.

'Hades, I am so sick of not knowing anything, of others making decisions about my life without me being involved, and being told there's no choice.'

'I'm sorry. I'm so sorry. I shouldn't have left you.'

'I *couldn't* have left you,' she whispered, her face a mask of betrayal.

'Well, apparently nor could I,' I snapped, rubbing my hands across my face. 'I don't know how many I killed. Most are demons who will regenerate.' Many weren't. Self-loathing roiled through my gut.

'Then why do it? Why did you leave me?'

I closed my eyes and let out a long breath. I had to make her understand. I couldn't let her think I didn't love her. I couldn't.

'You must never meet Cronos,' I said eventually, opening my eyes. She frowned.

'The titan in Tartarus?'

Apprehension and fear clouded her face and I reached for her again. She took my hand hesitantly, and a spark of something thrummed through my skin.

'Persephone, you can take power from others. If you were to take too much, from a far stronger being, you would not be able to hold onto it.'

'I don't understand.'

'There's no easy way to say this. Cronos is trapped, his power severely limited in Tartarus. If he were to use you as a vessel to channel his power...' I trailed off.

'What? What would happen?' Her eyes were filled with fear now.

'Your body would expel the magic,' I said tightly, rage and terror bubbling up again at the thought. 'Destroying you and everything around you.'

'You're telling me I'm a fucking bomb?'

'No. Only if you take the power of something exceptionally strong.'

'Like you?' she whispered. I shook my head.

'No. Stronger. Cronos is one of the original Titans, born of the sky and earth themselves. He is primordial in strength. You would be using his own power to destroy Tartarus.'

'Wouldn't that destroy him too?'

'A god can't be killed by their own power.'

She let out a long breath, then sat down beside me. I'd been so dazed that I hadn't even taken in my surroundings, and only then did I realize that we were in my own bedchamber, sitting on my bed.

'Is that why Poseidon hates me? Why he thinks I'm dangerous?' asked Persephone, her voice small. I looked back to her, noticing she was still wearing the red ballgown, scorched and torn.

'Yes.'

'Why didn't you tell me all this before? I would never have tried to get my powers back,' she said. 'If I didn't have my vines, there would be no risk of Cronos using them.'

'If I had told you this before, you would have been overwhelmed. And by the time you had eaten the first seed it was too late.'

'Take my powers away again,' she said, her eyes wide.

'No. I'm never leaving you again. If you become Queen of the Underworld, you must have your powers back, or you would not survive here. And...' I reached out, cupping her cheek in my hand. 'And I need your magic. You are the only one who can save me, Persephone.'

FOUR

PERSEPHONE

H ades' words reverberated through all the other thoughts ricocheting around my brain. *'You're the only one who can save me.'*

I knew it was true. I was the light to his dark, the balm to his pain, the healer of his shattered soul. The invisible connection to him burned hot inside me, and the desire to help him, heal him, take away all his pain, was overwhelming.

'Could... could you love a monster?' he asked me, hesitantly. I stared into his eyes, the question stirring emotions I had never, ever felt before. I pictured him as I'd just seen him, towering and blue and fearsome, the poisonous cruelty pouring into me through my vines.

But that wasn't him.

'No. I couldn't love a monster. But I could love you.' He gripped my hand harder, his angular face pinched and more fearful than I thought he could look.

'You have seen what is inside me,' he whispered.

'And I charge you to never let it win again. I will do whatever it takes to help you, Hades. You carry a burden heavier than most, but it does not define you.'

I was vaguely aware of the commitment I was making with my words, but they left my lips anyway, and the bond between us swelled and burned even hotter inside me. I knew with utter certainty that I had to be where Hades was. For as long as I lived, I needed to be by his side. He was my home. He was everything.

'I love you, Persephone,' he said, and his silver eyes were shining, all traces of melancholy gone.

I had never loved a man before, and I had nothing to compare what I was feeling with, but there was no doubt in my mind that this intense need for him to be happy, the need for him to be safe and with me always, was love.

'I love you,' I told him, and we moved together, our lips meeting.

Sparks of pleasure burst from the contact, his tongue seeking out mine with a sense of urgency that I relished. I needed him. I needed to show him how much I wanted him, needed there to be no gap between us, no distance for doubt or fear to fill.

His hands moved to my face, fingers caressing my cheek, then running through my tangled hair. I wrapped my own arms around his neck, deepening the kiss, heat and moisture pooling between my legs. Then he moved quickly, one arm around my back and the other under my legs, scooping me up into his arms. I gave a little squeak and he beamed at me, eyes gleaming with lust and promise.

'A bath, for my Queen,' he said huskily, and stood up. I kissed his jaw and neck as he carried me across the lavish room, and was rewarded with a strained grunt. I moved my kisses lower, across his collarbone. I could feel little sparks of pleasure through my whole body every time my lips met his skin. Was that the bond? If kisses felt this good... 'If you keep doing that I'll take you against that wall, and that's not how I want our first time to be,' he ground out, and I looked up at him.

'As long as you take me, I don't care,' I said, surprised at how husky my own voice sounded. I had wanted him for what seemed like forever, and I was ready. He gave a small growl, then kicked open a door in front of us. I gazed around at what looked like a freaking palace made of marble, slowly realizing it was a washroom. The bath was no ordinary bath though, it was a pool set into the stone floor, fed by a wall of quietly cascading water. A unit with two sinks and a long, ornate mirror lined the other wall.

Hades set me down on my feet, and stepped back from me, folding his arms across his bare chest.

'You can't bathe in your dress,' he said. Excitement quivered through me, making me ache.

'You'll need to undo it for me,' I answered, turning my back to him. Painfully slowly, he untied the lacing at the back, the bodice loosening around me.

'Done,' he grunted, and I turned back to him. The movement was enough to cause the loosened dress to drop to the floor around my feet, and his lips parted as he took in a breath.

'You are so beautiful,' he said. I knew he meant it, and confidence surged through me as I hooked my thumbs into the sides of my panties and slid them down. 'So, so beautiful,' he breathed, his eyes fixed between my thighs. Then they shot back up to mine, and he gave me a wicked grin as he snapped his fingers.

His jeans vanished.

I barely kept my footing as my gaze locked on him, hard and ready and freaking *glorious*. Desire was pounding at me now, slick and hot and untamable. But before I could throw myself at him he had scooped me up again, and was walking into the pool. Pleasure fizzed out from every point of contact our bare skin made, and I let out a wobbly moan of pleasure as hot water lapped at my skin as he moved deeper into the pool.

He set me on my feet once more when I was chest deep, the water moving against my hard nipples, then a bar of soap appeared in his hand. I cocked my head, about to ask him what he was doing but he spoke first.

'I want to wash away the horrors of this day, and give you some much, much better memories,' he said. Then he closed the gap between us, his soapy hands brushing over my shoulders, my back, down to my waist... I tensed with pleasure as his hands roamed, and when they reached my breasts he moved his head down and kissed me, my moan lost against his lips. His tongue flicked against mine in time with his fingers over my body and I willed them lower. The desire to feel him was now unstoppable, and I ran my hands over my own body, covering them in the foamy lather, then planted them on his rock hard abs. I felt him tense, his movements pausing for a split second, then speeding up, his finger and thumb now pinching at my nipples, causing pulses of painful pleasure in my core. I moved my hands down faster too, delighting in the feel of his solid muscles, his powerful body, the thought of everything he could do with it... My fingers moved under the water at his navel, and I soon felt coarse hair. Excitement made my breathing shallow, and I broke the kiss off to gulp down air, but as my fingers closed around him he kissed me again, hard and fierce.

I moved my hand along him in awe, and he suddenly wrapped one arm around the small of my back and lifted me from the pool floor. I gasped as he put his other hand under my leg, lifting me higher and making me let go of him to cling to his neck, wrapping my thighs around his waist. His hard length was pressed against me, and I gripped him tightly, leaning close to his ear.

'Take me. Please.'

'Tell me I'm yours,' he growled.

'I'm yours and you are mine.'

He lowered me slightly, and fiery pleasure spasmed through me as I felt him at my entrance.

'I'm yours and you are mine,' I repeated into his neck, almost delirious with need.

He lowered me again, pushing and stretching me exquisitely slowly.

'Once more,' he gasped, and I moved in his arms to look deep into his eyes.

'I'm yours and you are mine,' I breathed, and watched his eyes cloak with desire before he lowered me fully onto him. I threw my head back, crying out as my body clamped around him, filling me almost to the point of pain, but not quite. He moaned as his strong arms lifted me again, and shuddering pleasure rolled through me, obliterating everything but him.

Each time he moved me up and down I lost more of myself to his body, my mind taken over completely by the unbelievable feeling of rightness, the mounting power building inside me, growing with every thrust. It wasn't long before my whole body felt like it was alight with ecstasy, each time he filled me becoming more sure I would lose control.

'I love you, Persephone' he gasped, and I let go completely, my orgasm crashing through my body. He cried out and tensed, and I pressed myself against him, kissing him hard as he came, my core still hammered by waves of pleasure.

Slowly the water around us stilled, and Hades pushed his hand into my hair, pressing my heaving chest to his as I shuddered.

'You were made for me,' I told him, my voice breathless.

'Yes,' he said, and kissed me softly as he lifted me off him, back to unsteady feet. 'We were made for each other.'

. . .

He led me to the wall of cascading water, where we showered, soaping and stroking each other's bodies like greedy teenagers. When we were done, he carried me back to his bedroom, and laid me gently on the massive draped bed. I looked around the room curiously. Like Hecate's, it was dark and elegant, with imposing dark-wood furniture and soft black fabric. But as I looked up, I gave a little gasp of surprise. Instead of the starry rock ceiling in my own rooms, his was glowing with golden vines.

'So I always think of you, last thing at night and first thing in the morning,' he said, laying down beside me.

'How did I spend so many years not even knowing you existed?' I murmured, stroking my fingers down his stubbled jaw.

'I'm sorry,' he said.

'You need to stop saying that. I've forgiven you.' And it was true. I still hated a hundred or more things about Olympus, but I knew that whatever Hades had done, he had done it for me.

'I promise I will never leave you again,' he said, raw intensity making his voice thick.

'Good,' I said, and happiness blossomed in my chest. 'Now, I believe you said something about worshiping me?'

'You wish is my command, my Queen,' he said, the wicked gleam back in his eyes.

He rolled on top of me quickly, the feel of his hot skin making mine burst to life with tingles. I stared up at his beautiful, godly body and he licked his lips slowly. I squirmed.

'I recall you telling me you would make me forget my own name,' I ventured, my breath half held.

'So I did,' he answered, and lowered his head. He took my nipple in his mouth, nibbling and sucking, and I arched into him, instantly ready for him again. He kissed his way down my stomach, trails of heated sensation burning in his wake. When he reached the apex of my thighs he slowed, his tongue teasing me, as he kissed and nipped the tops of my thighs, coming dangerously close but never quite there.

'Please,' I panted, and his beautiful eyes flashed, before his tongue finally settled right between my legs. 'Oh good gods,' I moaned as I sank back, pleasure consuming me.

He was right. A few minutes later, I couldn't have told anyone my name if my life had depended on it.

FIVE

PERSEPHONE

W e made love over and over, neither one of us able to get enough of the other. Every time the uncomfortable thought of Tartarus or the Trials entered my head, I kissed him instead of voicing my fears, and he kissed me back like there was nothing in the world more important. He made me feel incredible. He made me feel like I was worth a thousand times what I had spent most of my life believing I was. He made me feel like a queen.

And I was discovering that the advantages of being with a god went further than mind-blowing sex. Whenever we were hungry or thirsty, he snapped his fingers and whatever we wanted appeared out of nowhere. From coffee to cake, if I craved it, he made it happen.

'You know, we're going to have to face the other gods soon,' I said as I lifted a cup of deliciously hot coffee to my lips.

'They can go fuck themselves,' answered Hades, his eyes flashing dangerously. 'You're staying.'

'Then you'll have to try to be diplomatic about it. Will they make the rest of the Trials harder for me?'

'Probably, yes. But you must win them.'

'What if I don't?' I didn't want to ask the question, but I had to. 'What if I lose? Will I be sent back?'

'I don't know, but I would be forced to marry Minthe.' Rage instantly flared inside me, and I felt the black vines pushing at my palms.

'Not a chance,' I hissed.

'Then you must win.' He leaned over and took my hand, and I forced myself to keep my eyes on his, instead of flicking down his delectable naked body.

'Right. No pressure then,' I said. A thought occurred to me abruptly. 'I was never judged after the last Trial.'

'No. That will have to be rectified.' He let out a long breath, and squeezed his fingers around mine. 'Persephone, you must be careful. We still do not know who is behind these macabre gifts you've been getting, or how you ended up in Tartarus. Zeus swears he had meant to send you to his own realm, and I believe him. Even he is not so stupid to play games with stakes that high.'

'You're going to lock me in my room for the rest of the Trials, aren't you?' I said, with a sad smile.

'No. I'm going to lock you in mine,' he grinned back at me.

'Well, that doesn't sound so bad.' I set my coffee down on the bedside table, and began to kiss him, but we were almost immediately interrupted.

'Hades! You are required at Mount Olympus. Now!'

The voice ripped through the bedchamber, and we both jumped. Hades' face darkened.

'He is the only one who can do that,' he growled. 'None of the others can get through my defenses.'

'Zeus?' I guessed, gulping. Hades nodded. 'Does he know I'm here?'

'Possibly. We shall go together.'

We dressed quickly, Hades conjuring up my fighting leathers for me. I gripped his hand tightly as he asked me if I was ready. I nodded, and with a bright flash, we were standing in Zeus' throne room, atop the mountain.

Zeus had not known I was back. That much was clear from the shock on the Lord of the God's face. He was enormous in his throne, purple light sparking around him and a lightning storm in his eyes. He was almost painful to look at, and I realized with trepidation that he had been ready for a fight with his brother.

'What is she doing here?' the sky god barked.

'She will finish the Trials,' Hades said, and let go of my hand as he grew. Pale blue light began to shimmer around him and I looked between him and Zeus, concern trembling through me. A fight between these two would be epic. And probably lethal for anyone not an Olympian.

'I heard you caused the death of sixty citizens. Explain yourself.' A sick feeling gripped my stomach as I looked at Hades. He had killed sixty people? *No, the monster had. Not him. He will never lose control again if you are with him.* I clung to the thought.

'I don't know how you came across that information, but what I do with prisoners in my own realm is no concern of yours,' Hades spat.

'Everything you do has become a concern of mine, brother. You can not be trusted.' Zeus' eyes were narrowed, his voice full of malice.

'You brought her back, Zeus. You started this, and now you will see it through to the end. I will call for the judging of the last Trial immediately.' The finality in Hades' voice carried a razor-sharp edge and the two gods stared at one another, tension crackling in the air. I scrabbled in my mind for some way to help, but Zeus spoke.

'I agree that she should finish the Trials. Call the judges.' I blinked, my mouth falling open. Hades stilled beside me, then slowly began to shrink to his usual size.

'I wasn't expecting him to back down so easily. What's going on?' I sent the thought to Hades silently, and his eyes flicked to mine.

'Zeus can hear everything we say like this in his realm,' he replied mentally. I looked at Zeus, alarmed, and he smiled at me.

'My realm, my rules,' he said with a shrug, and shimmered into the guy from the coffee shop. With a wave of his arm, his dais extended, and eleven other thrones materialized, then with a flash, the other gods appeared. I couldn't help glancing at Poseidon first, his face darkening with fury as he saw me.

'What is she doing here? I thought you took her back?' he hissed.

'She will finish the Trials,' said Hades, holding Poseidon's furious gaze. With a snarl, Poseidon sat down. Hades glanced at me, reassurance in his eyes, then strode towards his own throne at the end of the row.

'This is folly, Hades,' Poseidon called after him.

I couldn't help the fluttering feeling in my gut that the sea god was right. Wouldn't I want to get rid of someone who could accidentally end the world?

Now that I was out of the bubble of lust-induced bliss that was Hades' bedroom, the reality of what I had learned was beginning to sink in properly.

Someone had deliberately sent me to Tartarus. To Cronos. So whoever it was must know that my power was a way for Cronos to escape, and destroy Virgo. And if Virgo fell and Cronos was free, the rest of Olympus would not be far behind. Surely few people held that kind of knowledge? I looked at each of the gods in turn, trying to keep my suspicion from my face.

When my eyes landed on Zeus, I remembered that whilst I was on Mount Olympus he could read every one of my thoughts. Holding his gaze, I conjured up the thought of me punching him in the face, landing my fist on his nose repeatedly. He let out a low chuckle.

'Good day, Olympus! Due to an unexpected turn of events, we were not able to share Persephone's last test with you, and the judging was slightly delayed. But we are here with the little lady herself now, and the judges are ready!'

My vines itched at my palms as the intensely irritating commentator beamed at me from where he had appeared at the foot of the dais. I threw him a glare, before turning to where I knew the judges would be behind me. I was momentarily distracted by the breathtaking view of the clouds beyond them, but the commentator's voice sliced through my awe.

'Radamanthus?'

'You will lose one token.' Anger frittered through me. It wasn't my damned fault I couldn't complete Zeus's test, why should I lose a seed?

'Aeacus?'

'You will lose one token,' the pale judge said, nodding seriously. I clenched my teeth tightly.

'Minos?'

'You must lose one token, Persephone.' I could have sworn that there was the hint of an apology in the last judge's wise, dark eyes, but I glared at him all the same, until he vanished with the other two judges. The seed box was suddenly in my hand, hard and real. I'd won four tokens, and eaten two. I sighed as I opened the box slowly. One of the two remaining, perfectly-preserved seeds vibrated in the box, then vanished.

At least I hadn't lost any of my power, I told myself. And there were still three Trials to go. Minthe ended the Trials with five seeds, and I still had three. If I won all my remaining Trials, I could still win. I *had* to win. There was no way I could watch Hades marry another woman, least of all Minthe. Just thinking about her in his bed made my insides twist, a guttural sense of wrongness spreading through me. I shook the thoughts from my head, trying to focus.

'So the lovely Persephone loses one token, leaving her with three. Tomorrow we'll find out what's in store for her next, when we start Round Three of the Hades Trials!' The commentator beamed at me, before the world flashed.

I blinked around at my own room, relief washing through me as I saw Hades standing beside me.

'Hey, why couldn't you flash us out of Tartarus like that?' I asked, turning to him as the question struck me. 'Why did I have to touch you?'

'Because I was using just about all the strength I had to hold back Cronos. My power couldn't reach you.' His voice was hard and angry, and I stood up on tiptoes to kiss his cheek. His expression softened instantly.

'Well, thanks for rescuing me.' He brought his hand to my jaw, tilting my head towards him. But just as he leaned forward to kiss me, a male voice ripped through the moment.

'Persy, what the fuck is going on?' I spun to see my brother crashing through my bedroom door, his face white, and an exasperated Hecate behind him.

'You took arriving in Olympus a shitload better than he's taking it,' she said to me, following him into the room and holding the door open a moment. Skop bounded into

the room, and a smile split my face. Hecate kicked the
door shut and folded her arms across her chest as Sam
froze, his eyes flicking between the little dog and Hades.

'Hey Skop!' I said, as the kobaloi leaped up onto the
bed, his tail wagging furiously.

*'I'm really, really glad you're back, Persy. Hades is a
dick for taking you away.'*

'Thanks Skop. I'm glad too, but it wasn't Hades' fault,'
I said to him silently. *'We've made up.'* I couldn't keep the
heat from my cheeks and Skop barked.

'You banged him! At last!'

'Persy!' Sam's urgent words snapped my attention
back to him. He and Hades were staring at each other,
more and more black smoke billowing from Hades' skin.

'No, don't put the smoke up!' I said quickly, laying my
hand on his arm. 'Please, let him see you. He's my
brother. He's called Sam.' I looked at Sam. 'And this is
Hades.' Sam moved his mouth a few times, but nothing
came out. 'This is Skop, and you've already met Hecate,' I
continued. I was feeling guilty that I'd been holed up
with Hades in a lust bubble for hours, when my brother
had been somewhere in the Underworld, clearly freaking
out. Although it sort of served him right for not believing
me.

'Erm,' he said eventually.

'Nice to meet you,' said Hades stiffly.

'We shake hands in my world,' I prompted him.

'I'm a god and a king,' he said, looking at me. 'People
bow to me, not shake my hand.'

'I know, but he's my brother and he's a little bit

shocked. It might be easier to ease him into the god/king thing.' Hades looked from me to Sam, then reluctantly held out his hand. Sam stared at it for a few seconds, then stumbled forward and took it.

'You were telling the truth,' he whispered, looking at me.

'Yeah,' I nodded.

'Does that mean you really have magic powers?' His voice was filled with awe, and I looked at Hecate.

'How much have you told him? I'd have thought he'd be at least a little used to the idea of Olympus by now.'

'I haven't told him anything. He was irritating me, so I had Hypnos put him to sleep,' she shrugged. I closed my eyes and clenched my jaw a moment as Hades dropped Sam's hand.

'Hecate, not that I'm not grateful to see my brother, but why did you bring him here?'

'He said I was outrageously hot.'

'That is not a good reason,' said Hades.

'*It's a fucking excellent reason,*' said Skop.

I sighed.

As if I didn't already have enough to deal with.

SIX

PERSEPHONE

I asked Hades to conjure some nectar, and once Sam was sitting down, with the reinforcing drink working its way through his system, he was a lot easier to talk to. I couldn't help the beam of satisfaction I got from the amazement in my big brother's face when I showed him my vines. Usually Sam was the impressive one. He'd gotten a great job building apps for cell phones, completely self-taught, and had been the one to finally improve my parents' living space from the shitty trailer we'd grown up in, to an RV.

But as much as I loved him for that, I couldn't deny that it felt good to be the impressive sibling for a change.

I showed him how the vines changed color and told him about the conservatory and how I could grow plants, although I left out the part about my gold vines. I did not want to talk about magic sex powers with my own brother.

I told him about the Trials so far, Hades' face darkening with anger the more I spoke, and Sam's a mask of horror by the time I'd finished. With Hecate and Skop there though, I didn't mention what Hades had told me about Cronos and Tartarus. I wasn't sure if they were supposed to know about it. Hell, I wasn't sure I *wanted* them to know about it. Being a walking, talking bomb that could destroy their world wasn't exactly something I wanted to share.

'So... Now you have to do three more Trials, and win them all to marry Hades?'

'Yes.'

'And...' His eyes flicked between me and Hades. 'Do you want to marry him?' He whispered the question. I felt a wave of heat come from Hades, and couldn't suppress my smile. What in the world did Sam think he could do to stop Hades if I didn't want to marry him? I loved him for asking though.

'Winning the Trials is certainly the best option I have right now. At least if I win, I have a choice,' I said carefully. More heat rolled off Hades.

'You know, I only just decided that I'm in love with you. You can't just assume I want to marry you already,' I told Hades in my mind. I made my tone teasing, but there was an element of truth in the words. Being parted from him would be worse than death. It would be tortuous.

But I'd literally only slept with him that day. Marriage commitments seemed a little premature.

'You are mine,' Hades said in my mind.

'Yes. Body and soul,' I answered. The air cooled. *'But*

where I come from you don't just claim people if you want to marry them. We should discuss this later.'

'*Fine,*' he grunted.

'Sam, now that you know I'm safe, I think Hecate should take you back to New York,' I said, sitting down beside him on my bed and looking pointedly at Hecate.

'No way! You're safe right now, but you've got three more of these Trials to do!'

'And how would you help me?' I asked him gently. 'You're in more danger than I am here, you have no powers.'

'I'm not leaving you to these maniacs,' he said stubbornly. Another wave of heat rolled off Hades.

'Sam, you could be used against me. In my first Trial they nearly killed Skop because they knew I cared for him. Imagine what they would do to my own brother?'

'I can handle it.'

'No, you can't. When we first arrived here the sight of Hades in full god form caused you to black out. It nearly killed me, before I had my power.'

'He nearly killed you?' Sam gaped at me. 'And you're fucking considering marrying him?'

'It's not as simple as that!'

'Persy, I'm staying. If I can't help you physically, then at least I might be able to talk some sense into you.' He folded his arms, eyes fierce.

I sighed. Hades was staying eerily quiet. I turned to him.

'Can he stay just a little while?' Hades stared at me,

silver eyes a swirling mass of tension. He turned to Hecate abruptly.

'You caused this mess. Clean it up,' he said to her. I opened my mouth but he carried on. 'Persephone will be moving into my rooms. He can have this room. If he leaves it once without you, I'm giving your job to that fucking skull you care for.'

'Yes boss,' Hecate said, flashing a wicked grin at me as my brother spluttered. My cheeks heated.

'You're staying in his rooms?' Sam half whispered at me, the disbelief back.

'Yep,' I said, my voice coming out awkwardly high-pitched.

This had to be the worst brother-boyfriend introduction ever.

My new living arrangements caused a raft of arguments. Sam kicked up such a row about being locked in the windowless bedroom on his own that eventually Hecate gave up and told him he could sleep on her sofa. None of us told him there were no windows in her rooms either.

Convincing Hades to let Skop stay with me in his rooms was a harder task. The little dog didn't make it any easier, hurling insults about the King of the Underworld into my head the entire time I begged Hades to let him come with me.

'He is the spy of another god, Persephone, you don't know how much you ask of me,' Hades said, exasperated.

Guilt trickled through me as I recalled Hecate telling me how secretive Hades was about his realm.

'But he's one of my only friends here, and he's helped save my life,' I said. 'Plus he already knows loads about Virgo now. It's not like he'll be with you all the time, he'll be with me, and I'm not allowed to go anywhere or do anything.'

'*Fuck no. I'll be with him as little as possible,*' said Skop in my head.

'*You're lucky he bans mind-reading, now behave your-self!*' I snapped back at the kobaloi.

'He must sleep in the antechamber, and he must hear none of our conversations,' Hades growled eventually.

'Thank you!' I squeaked, and flung my arms around his neck. His tense shoulders relaxed under my embrace, and my brother made a strangled sound.

'You are welcome,' Hades said, but he didn't sound like he meant it. 'Now regretfully, I must go. I have neglected my duties and have a lot to... attend to.' I could see the guilt and pain in his face, felt his shame through the bond, and my heart ached for him. He could not escape the consequences of his wrath.

Had he saved me from facing mine when I drank from the river Lethe and forgot whatever it was I had done? Fresh frustration clouded my mind at the thought. I was fast reaching a point where I wanted to believe Hades was right about me being better off not knowing what I had done in the past. I had enough shit to wade through already, with the Trials and Cronos and

Tartarus. Did I really need to know anymore? Would any good come of it?

How can you not know what you are capable of? Of course you need to know. The voice inside me was inescapable, and it was a blend of fear and justice. Whether I needed punishing or forgiving for my actions, both were important.

'Kerato will have regenerated soon,' said Hecate, and a small sound of relief escaped me as her words cut through my thoughts. The minotaur was OK.

'Tell him thank you from me, will you?' I said to Hades.

'Of course. I will see you in a few hours.' He leaned down to kiss me softly, then vanished. I felt a small pang of loss, but the bond flared inside me, reassuring and bright. I turned to Sam, determined to keep my mind off the myriad concerns rolling around my brain.

'Right. There are a few things you need to know about the Underworld. Hecate? Help me out?'

Hecate had barely begun telling Sam about the twelve realms when the world flashed around me.

Panic engulfed me, every frazzled part of me expecting to come face to face with the flaming river of Tartarus and my vines tore from my palms before the light had even cleared from my eyes.

But the scene that came into focus before me wasn't

dark and fiery at all. It was bright and warm and breezy. And beautiful.

'Zeus?'

I was in the breakfast room on Zeus's mountain.

'I wouldn't try using those vines on me,' his voice sounded behind me. I whirled, and gasped. He was shirt-less, in the older, dignified form I'd seen him in a few times before. And this close it was impossible not to see how much better it was than the blond surfer boy form. If the angles of his face, the corded muscle across his chest, and the tightness of his abs weren't enough to make my breath catch, then the gleam in his eyes was. He oozed sex. Like it was actually pouring from his body.

'Stop. Now. I was told gods weren't allowed do this,' I said.

'I have no idea what you mean,' he said, stepping closer to me. I stepped backwards. 'I've brought you here to talk with you. On matters of grave importance.' He licked his lips, and my chest heaved. *Focus, Persephone!*

'You told me you wanted me to win last time I was here. Why?'

'Because my brother is not the god he used to be. The Underworld has changed him.'

'You did that to him, not the Underworld!'

'We all have our burdens, Persephone. Do you think it is easy for me to control the skies?'

'I don't believe it is as hard as controlling the dead,' I retorted. Zeus tilted his head, regarding me.

'I'll admit Leo has some benefits over Virgo,' he said

eventually. 'Come with me.' He held out his hand, and I shook my head.

'No.' My left foot moved against my will. 'Bastard,' I snarled.

'I won't make you do any more than move your feet, feisty little goddess,' he smiled at me, then gripped my hand. With another flash we were gone from the mountain, standing instead on wooden planks. Wind suddenly rushed across me, blowing my hair around my face. We were moving, and as I looked around myself I stumbled. We were on a ship, and the sails billowing in front of me were shining like metallic liquid. Clouds flew past us on either side, spirals of glittering dust corkscrewing through the sky.

An overwhelming sense of freedom filled me, and I held my arms out as we soared through the sky. I felt like my worries were peeling away from me in the cool wind, the past, future and everything in between paling against the bliss.

With an abrupt flash, the wind stopped, and I blinked around at a courtyard garden. I gazed up at the most incredible trellis, covered in roses of every color I could imagine, the thorns shining gold.

'Beautiful, aren't they?'

'Yes,' I breathed, turning. Zeus was standing in front of a tall fountain, dragonflies the size of birds darting above his head. I could see Mount Olympus behind him, more of the flying ships cruising around it. 'Where are we?'

'One of the mansions that ring Mount Olympus. You created them.'

'What?'

'The gold-thorned roses. You created them.' I blinked at him, and he laughed softly. 'Olympus may have forgotten you, Persephone, but you left a legacy deeper than even Hades knows.'

'Why have you brought me here?'

'You need to know that the Underworld is not the only place that would welcome you.'

I frowned at him.

'You're trying to... make friends with me?'

'You are not meant to be kept underground, Persephone. You were born of light and nature. Not darkness and death.' Fear started to prick at the calm enveloping me. He was right. No matter my feelings for Hades, I couldn't live in Virgo. I couldn't live in the darkness, with that barren landscape the closest thing to nature I could get to.

'Are you telling me I can visit places like this when I am Queen of the Underworld?' I asked, a sick feeling in my stomach. That wasn't what he was telling me, and I knew it wasn't.

'No, Persephone. I'm telling you that you were never meant to be Queen of the Underworld. A Queen, yes. But not of the dead.'

'I love Hades,' I said, the words flying to my lips.

'I don't doubt it. But that doesn't change the fact that you can't live in the Underworld. Look at what it has done to Hades. And he is much, much stronger than you will ever be.'

No... No, I had to be with Hades. But he was bound to Virgo, he couldn't leave. Would the Underworld turn me into a monster like him? Was that what had happened before? Hecate's story burst into my mind.

'I can sacrifice something! Something important, to save my soul,' I said quickly.

'And be as miserable as that Titan witch your whole life?' Zeus' voice was low and he was moving closer to me. 'If you let me, Persephone, I can make you so much more.'

SEVEN

PERSEPHONE

Zeus' magic rolled over me, the sweet scent of roses, the kiss of the breeze, the heat of his body, all consuming my rational thoughts.

'More than what?' I asked, my pulse racing. 'What can you make me?'

'Anything you want to be. A goddess without constraints, a goddess living in the light.' His words were like a caress, and I stared into his purple eyes.

'A goddess living in the light,' I repeated breathlessly. How could I live any other way? I couldn't, *wouldn't* spend my life in the dark. Hades' own words filtered through my mind.

'You can't keep a light this bright in the dark.'

But I couldn't live without Hades either. Confusion was pouring through me in rivers as the terrible realization began to settle over me. This was why the idea of marriage had unsettled me. This was why my head was refusing to process a future with Hades, was putting off the decision until after the Trials. Because I couldn't live in the Underworld with him. I couldn't live in the dark.

What had I done? I'd let the bond awaken, let myself fall in love with a man I couldn't be with, with a man who needed me for his soul to survive. I would destroy both of us if I left, but the thought of those rock walls, the Empusa's lair, the fiery river of Tartarus and its tortured souls, the empty, barely-lit landscape... It would take my soul, I realized, tears burning hot behind my eyes yet again. The longer I stayed in that place, the more of my soul would die. It might take a hundred years, or a thousand, but my soul would eventually be lost to the darkness.

'Persephone, let me show you the life you should live. Let me show you what you truly deserve.'

'What do I have to do?'

'Win the Trials. Prove you are worthy of a crown. And when I tell the world you will be Queen of a brand new realm, *your own* realm, a realm filled with light and life and nature, you must stand by my side.'

A new realm? Was he talking about the realm Hades had created and was being punished for? I gaped at Zeus, the reality of what he was saying crashing through me as Hades' pain-filled face dominated my thoughts.

'You hate him that much?'

Zeus' smile slipped.

'You hate him enough to get the woman he loves to leave him and rule the realm he created to replace her? You cruel, cruel, vicious bastard!' I was yelling suddenly, all calm abandoning me and a rage gripping me in its place. Black vines leapt from my palms, snaking towards Zeus. 'You fear him, Zeus. You underestimated his power, and now you fear you can't control him.'

The sky god's expression twisted, his beautiful face suddenly ugly with anger.

'He was only able to create that realm because of that Titan bitch,' he hissed. 'He's not that strong, and don't let him pretend otherwise. You could be stronger.'

'No, Zeus. I could not. And I would rather spend one day with him than an eternity without. I will be strong by his side, and I will make him stronger. And together you will be no match for us.'

Within a second he was three times his normal size, fizzing purple lightning flashing around him. Thunder crashed overhead, but my vines didn't recoil. They grew with him, whipping around me.

I wasn't scared of him. The realization buoyed me, and I pictured Hades standing behind me, his strength and love flowing into me.

'Are you threatening me, flower goddess?' boomed Zeus.

'Yes. Stay the fuck away from Hades. You've done enough.'

He laughed, a great, booming cackle.

'If I didn't respect you so much, I would smite you where you stand! You, who can just about make plants grow and throw some vines around, are trying to protect the King of the Underworld, one of the three most powerful beings in Olympus?' I opened my mouth to tell him that the Titans were stronger than him, but he began to shrink down quickly, and I faltered, surprised.

He was smiling, I saw, as he reached human size, the purple magic around him dissipating.

'I believe you have passed, Persephone,' he said, the wicked gleam back in his eyes. 'But you really did anger me there. You walk a fine line. Threaten me again, and I will end you.'

'Passed? What the fuck are you talking about?' I said, confused enough to ignore his threat.

Hera appeared beside him in a flash of turquoise, and my vines disintegrated as I looked between them.

'You have just passed the loyalty Trial, Persephone,' Hera said. I blinked at her. 'Well done. Hades will be lucky to have you if you can win the rest of the competition.'

EIGHT

HADES

Persephone was opening and closing her mouth, confusion and fury on her face, as she was flashed into my throne room. I couldn't stop the black smoke around me vibrating, anger causing the beast inside me to growl.

One day I would be able to stop Zeus. One day he wouldn't be able to play with me like I was his fucking toy. But right now... The Trials were overruling my command in my own realm, leaving him to do whatever the fuck he pleased with Persephone, with the backing of the other Olympians.

Like abducting her from her own rooms and forcing her to realize that she couldn't live in the Underworld with me.

Pain sliced through the anger and a wave of heat rippled out from me as Persephone's eyes snapped to mine. Slow realization was dawning on her face.

'You saw all of that,' she said inside my head as the

commentator appeared at the foot of the dais. It wasn't a question, and her mental voice was strained. I swallowed my anger and replied.

'Yes. And I have never loved you more.'

'I'm sorry. I'm sorry I even considered his words, his magic is so strong, I-' I cut her off, unable to take the anguish in her voice.

'Very few can resist Zeus' power. And fewer still would outright threaten him. You sounded like a true Queen.'

'Good day, Olympus!' sang the commentator. Persephone turned to him. 'As you all just saw, little Persephone has successfully passed the loyalty test!' I flicked my eyes to Zeus, hatred bubbling through my veins. The world saw what he wanted them to see, not what had actually happened. There was no way he had let all of Olympus see Persephone standing up to him like that. Nor would he have broadcast any mention of the new realm. The only reason he had let us Olympians see what had really been said was because he wanted to taunt me, wanted me to see Persephone consider leaving or betraying me.

And although her fierce reaction had been more than I could have dreamed of, what Zeus had said was true, and Persephone knew it. She wasn't made for darkness and death. She would become muted and miserable as time went on, a shadow of herself. And it would be my fault. How could I let that happen?

Her words sang through my skull. *'I would rather*

spend one day with him than an eternity without. I will be strong by his side, and I will make him stronger. And together you will be no match for us.'

Love so powerful it made my chest hurt fired inside me, and her eyes snapped to me again, softer now. She felt my emotion, through the bond.

'So now, to the judges!' The commentator's voice severed the moment, and the judges shimmered into the room. In turn they each pronounced that Persephone had earned one token, then the seed box appeared in her hand. She held it as though it were toxic, rather than a prize.

Before she or I could say a word, Zeus waved his arm and the room emptied immediately, leaving just the Olympian gods in their thrones.

'Where have you sent her?' I barked, leaping to my feet.

'Relax, brother. I've put her back exactly where I found her.' His expression was one of boredom but there was a glint in his eyes that said otherwise. My fury deepened.

'This is my realm!' I bellowed. 'You do not dismiss my subjects, I do!'

'Now, now, Hades. I would have thought you'd be pleased. Persephone stood up to the King of the Gods for you,' said Hera, standing. 'That's really quite a feat.'

'And now she knows that she won't be happy here. She knows what the rest of Olympus has to offer in comparison.' I couldn't keep the bitterness from my voice.

A smug smile flashed across Zeus' face and my vision clouded. My monster was crawling its way up my chest, straining to get out.

'She loves you, Hades. If she wins the Trials this will be the best outcome you could have possibly hoped for,' Hera said.

'Unless she remembers what she did and loses her shit again,' added Zeus.

'Don't you dare,' I hissed. 'Her memories and the River Lethe are out of bounds for these Trials,' I spat, and I felt the temperature in the room plummet around me as I channeled my power.

'Agreed,' said Poseidon loudly.

'Agreed,' echoed Athena, Hermes and Dionysus. Relief tempered my anger a little. Zeus couldn't go against everyone. He shrugged diffidently.

'I wasn't suggesting that we did.'

My eyes flicked over the gods who had remained silent. I hadn't had any idea this damned Trial was happening, but in the short time I'd been alone I had been able to reach one vital conclusion.

Whoever was behind the macabre gifts Persephone had been getting must know what she had done before she drank from the river Lethe. And they must also be able to control the minds of the humans they were using to make up this Spring Undead faction. If they were also responsible for her unexpected trip to Tartarus then they knew about Cronos, which severely limited the list of suspects.

To the eleven gods in front of me.

·   ·   ·

All of them stared back, able to see through my smoke facade. Who would want to release the world's worst monster, Cronos, and start a new war, ending Olympian rule? Who would want to destroy Virgo? It made no sense. It had taken an age to build Olympus as it was now, countless fights and mistakes finally culminating in something they all benefited from.

I saw no reason why any of them would want to destroy it all. My gaze settled on Ares. Was he angry enough? Desperate for war enough? He glared back at me through the slits in his helmet.

The only thing I was sure of was that it wasn't either of my brothers. They had the most to lose.

'If you're not going to rant and rage and entertain me, then I'm leaving,' said Zeus, and before I could open my mouth he had gone. The others stood, Hermes and Aphrodite the only ones to nod at me politely before vanishing too. But one god stayed behind.

'How's Persy doing?' Dionysus asked.

'Why?' I snapped, suspicion filling me.

'Chill out, man, you know I care about her.' The wine god swiveled in his throne, kicking his leg up over the arm.

'You know exactly how she's doing, the kobaloi is keeping you well informed, I have no doubt.'

'Hmm,' grunted Dionysus, a goblet of wine appearing in his hand. 'Fancy a drink?'

'No.'

'Naked nymphs, you're dull. Get your ass over to one of my parties one day,' he said, and drained his goblet in one.

'I have work to do here, unlike the rest of you.'

'Hades, you have underlings. Share the load. You do not need to spend your whole life in a fucking cave. And nor does she,' he said.

'Coming from a god who lives in a tree,' I snorted.

'It's a very nice tree,' he said, standing up and stretching. 'And it's where she grew up. The first time.'

'What's your point, Dionysus? I am busy.'

'My point is that she doesn't have to live here for you two to be together.'

I scowled at him.

'You're saying she could live with you?'

'Yeah. She did before.'

'No.' The word had left my mouth before I had even considered the notion.

'She likes trees, man, she'd be happy-'

'I said no.'

The wine god's face hardened.

'It's not up to you. It's up to her.'

'Persephone is mine.' The words came out as a snarl, and blue light burst to life around me.

'Ease up, man, I know she is. I'm just trying to help,' Dionysus said, holding his hands up. But the fierce look in his eyes belied the casual words. 'Think about it,' he said, then disappeared.

As little as I wanted to, I found that I couldn't help thinking about what Dionysus had said. Persephone would love living on Taurus. It was nature and madness combined, a limitless island covered in giant plants and wild creatures. It was perfect for her. That's why Demeter had left her there.

I stopped by her room to make sure she was alright, but her brother was there, along with the kobaloi spy. In some ways I was relieved she wasn't alone. She had expressed her hatred for Virgo many times before, but now the subject had been laid so bare before us that we would have to talk about it. And I had no solutions. Only wildly conflicting emotions. The thought of making her suffer was intolerable. But so was the thought of living without her. Was visiting her on another realm whenever the Underworld could spare me really an option? In the early days I had tested the limits of my bind to Virgo, and found that I could never leave for long, or the monster became wild and even less tamable, and my control over the demons and Tartarus weakened.

I made my excuses and left, forcing myself to focus on more immediate problems. Persephone had two more Trials to survive and win, and she couldn't be sabotaged again. The thought of her in Tartarus made the monster roar within me, dark rage twisting my insides. I wanted to talk to Kerato about my suspicions. Every human member of the faction we had caught had known nothing about how their memories had returned, and if it was indeed a god directing them, then interrogating them further was pointless. We would learn nothing from them at all.

NINE

PERSEPHONE

'*You know, you can't avoid me forever.*' I sent the thought at Hades, hoping that wherever he was he could hear me.

'*I'm sorry. I have much to attend to,*' he replied immediately. '*Go to sleep, and we'll talk in the morning.*'

I blew out a sigh and lay back on his enormous bed. It felt too big without him in it, his mighty presence altering the scale of everything around me. Hecate had brought me to his rooms earlier, and now I'd had too much time alone to think.

Whilst I was incredibly relieved to have passed another Trial and won a seed, I couldn't suppress my anger at the gods. I'd been warned of the loyalty Trial, I knew I wouldn't see it coming, but to force me to admit in front of Hades that I didn't want to live in his realm? It was cruel beyond belief.

He had come by after the Trial but his face was strained, his manner awkward. I hadn't known what to say to him. My mind screamed against the notion of being trapped in the dark for eternity, but the feeling didn't outweigh my desire for him.

'The last two Trials are going to be the hardest,' said Skop, interrupting my thoughts.

'Huh,' I said, hugging my knees to my chest. 'If Hades catches you on the bed you are going to be in deep shit.'

'Persy, you should eat another seed. The more power you have, the more likely you'll survive. And win.'

'We'll find out what the Trial is first,' I said evasively. I didn't want more power. I didn't want to make myself stronger.

I was already dangerous enough.

I did fall asleep before Hades returned, and almost instantly found myself in the Atlas garden.

'Ah, little goddess,' the voice whispered across the breeze, as a delicious calm wrapped itself around me. The sunflowers had grown, they were now as tall as I was. I brushed my finger along their petals as I made my way across the soft turf to the fountain.

'I have a question for you,' I said.

'By all means.'

'Do you know how I ended up in Tartarus?'

There was a long silence from the voice, filled by the sound of birds tweeting.

'I did not know you had been to Tartarus. That is an unpleasant place,' the stranger said eventually.

'It is,' I replied, running my fingers through the warm

water and watching the lily-pads ripple. 'Will I die if I live in the Underworld forever?'

'No. Not if you are stronger than the evil there.'

'But if I become stronger, I become more dangerous.'

'Wrong. The stronger you are, the more control you have.'

'I want to stay in Olympus. But I don't want to live away from nature. It feels wrong.'

'That should not be your biggest concern now. You must regain your memories and right the injustice dealt to you. You must regain your power and learn who you are. Then you will know what is right or wrong. Then you will be able to make decisions about your future.'

I thought about that, the calm of the garden allowing the thoughts to organize themselves more clearly. It was true that the most urgent issue was surviving the Trials and discovering who had sent me to Tartarus. But did I need my memories back? Would it really help?

'What happens if I just stay ignorant? What if Hades and Athena are right?'

'Then you will forever be incomplete. Those who have used you, sought to harm you and Hades, will have won.'

Anger rumbled through me. Harm Hades? No. No, I couldn't allow that.

'Can't you just tell me what happened? Who my enemies are?'

'To know for sure, you must recover your memories. If you eat another seed, you will be able to find the river Lethe.'

. . .

The conversation was clear in my mind when I awoke, Skop still at the end of the bed and Hades nowhere to be seen.

'Where are you?' I projected at him groggily.

'I'm here,' he replied, and I sat up with a start. The voice hadn't been in my head, it had come from the adjoining room. I swung my legs out of bed, the only light coming from the softly glowing vines on the ceiling.

'Hades?' He was sitting shirtless in a large wingback chair, a tumbler of something amber in his hand. 'Are you OK?'

'I had a lot to clear up,' he said, his voice bitter.

'It wasn't you, don't forget that,' I said, padding over to him. He didn't answer, but I felt his body relax as I eased myself onto his lap. 'How's Kerato?'

'Good. It'll be a while before he's strong again, demons get stronger the longer they've been living.'

'Are all minotaurs demons?'

'No. Kerato became a demon to live here.' He looked at me as I wound my arms around his neck. 'Did Hecate tell you what she gave up in order to keep her soul?'

'Yes,' I nodded.

'Well, Kerato, and many others here, didn't have enough to give up. The Underworld owns them.'

'It doesn't own you,' I whispered. 'It owns the darkness inside you, but you are stronger.'

'*We* are stronger,' he corrected me, and kissed me gently. 'Persephone, Zeus was right. You could be so much more above ground. You are a nature goddess, with earth magic. This is no place for you.' The anguish in his words made the need to help him overtake my own concerns.

'I'll be fine,' I said. 'And anyway, I've decided not to think about it until after the Trials. My brain can only take so many life-threatening scenarios at a time, and the Trials are more urgent,' I said, thinking about what the stranger had said to me.

Guilt trickled through me at the thought of the Atlas garden. Should I tell Hades about it? It felt wrong keeping a secret from him, but as soon as I opened my mouth to speak, I closed it again.

Hades wouldn't tell me about my past, but the stranger wanted me to know. They were at odds. And I had first-hand evidence that Hades didn't always make the right decisions; he had felt obligated to take me back to New York when that was the worst thing he could possibly have done. He didn't necessarily know what was best for me, and until I knew what I wanted, it seemed a good idea to keep silent.

'I think focusing on the more immediate issues is a very good idea,' Hades said, and swigged from his glass. 'I believe the person who sent you to Tartarus was an Olympian.'

'You do?'

'Yes. Nobody else except my inner circle knows about Cronos.'

'What if whoever it is doesn't know about Cronos, and just hoped I'd die there? I mean, a trip to Tartarus is a pretty awful punishment, even if Cronos wasn't part of it.'

'No, it's too much of a coincidence.' I cocked my head.

'Hades, did Cronos have something to do with what happened before?'

'I swore to you I would never talk to you about what happened, please stop putting me through this,' he said tightly. *That wasn't a no.*

'Putting *you* through this?' I said indignantly. 'I think you'll find I'm the one being put through it.' I pushed my chin out, and he moved his hand to my jaw, stroking his thumb across my skin.

'I know. I'm sorry. Let me make it up to you?' His eyes were dark suddenly, and his chest was tensing. A wave of heat, smelling like wood-smoke, rolled over me and desire tingled through my whole body, my anger vanishing.

'I suppose I could be persuaded,' I mumbled, as he leaned forward and closed his lips over mine.

TEN

PERSEPHONE

'I must hold court today, I am days behind,' said Hades the next morning, rolling to the edge of the mattress and sitting up. I blinked the sleep from my eyes, and yawned.

'What do you do during court?'

'Judge the dead,' he muttered, his muscled back to me. I slowly pointed my palm at him, and a gold vine snaked out, creeping towards him.

'Sounds intense,' I said.

'Some days are worse than others. You should train with Hecate as much as you can today, and I'll see you at the Trial announcement tonight.' He started to stand, but my vines wrapped around his waist fast.

'Or I could see you some more now,' I grinned as I tugged.

His huge frame didn't move, and he twisted to look at me, a wicked gleam in his eyes.

'You're going to have to get much stronger than that if you want to move me,' he said.

'I don't need to move you physically,' I answered, and sent my power through my vine, recalling as much detail as I could from the night before. His eyes darkened instantly, and he stood up, turning towards me and giving me an eyeful of his now aroused naked body.

'I believe you win this one,' he murmured, and pounced.

Eventually he did leave, after filling the table in his living rooms with waffles and piping hot coffee for me. Again I felt the initial pang of panic at his loss, until the bond fired, reassuring and solid. I could definitely get used to never feeling completely alone, I thought as I tucked into my breakfast. I could get used to magic waffles too.

Hecate and Sam arrived half an hour later. Sam was almost alarmingly bright and enthusiastic compared to the day before and I eyed Hecate suspiciously.

'What have you given him?' She shrugged and Sam answered me.

'Just some coffee, we were up all night talking about Olympus. It sounds freaking awesome, have you seen the giant trees or the underwater cities?' He was talking fast and I raised an eyebrow.

'You sound like you've had about ten coffees.'

'A few, I guess. What are we doing today?'

'Erm, training. The next Trial is announced tonight.'

'Can I train too?'

'No,' Hecate and I said together.

'Oh.'

'Skop, can you talk to Sam in his head?' I asked, a thought occurring to me. The kobaloi didn't answer me but Sam's face changed suddenly, his eyes widening as he looked down at the dog. 'I'll take that as a yes,' I smiled. 'Sam, you can practice talking back to him. You have to project the thoughts to him, concentrating hard the whole time.'

'You can talk to the dog in your head?' Sam shook his head in disbelief. 'This place is crazy.'

'Actually, he's not a dog,' Hecate said. 'He's a kobaloi. Which is a shape-shifting sprite.' Sam looked at Skop.

'How come you choose to be a dog then?' he asked. With a little shimmer Skop shifted, his naked gnome body taking the furry dog's place. Sam's mouth slowly formed an O shape as he stared.

'Because I won't wear clothes and your sister didn't like this,' Skop answered, pointing with both hands at his genitals.

'Yeah, I can't say I blame her,' said Hecate. Skop grinned at me from under his beard before shifting back to dog form.

'There's a drinks thing tonight at the announcement,' Hecate said.

'Great,' I said, rolling my eyes. 'Poseidon can glare at me some more, and Zeus can march around being a prick.'

'You did well turning him down,' said Hecate. I cocked my head at her. 'I wanted to screw him from the other side of a flame dish, so the gods know how hard it must have been for you.'

'What did you see during the loyalty Trial?' I asked slowly.

'Him coming on to you, you saying no,' she shrugged.

'That wasn't what happened,' I said quietly. 'He didn't try to sleep with me, though he was definitely turning on the charm. He tried to get me to renounce living with Hades if I won the Trials.'

'Really?'

'Yeah. He said I could rule the new realm if I left Hades.'

'Fucking asshole,' spat Hecate.

'I know. I told him I would rather lose my soul to Virgo than leave Hades. And then I told him to fuck off and leave us alone, that together we would be strong enough to stand up to him.'

Hecate let out a long whistle, her eyes as wide as my brother's.

'No wonder they didn't broadcast that. Nice one.' I grinned at the pride I could see in her eyes.

'Yeah, well, he threatened to kill me if I made him angry again, so... making an enemy of the Lord of the Gods can be ticked off my to-do list.'

I trained hard with Hecate most of the day, and not just on dagger work and close combat. She set up archery targets on tall stands around the room, and I practiced launching my vines at precise points on the targets, as well as using them to lift and throw the structures.

I did OK, but I knew I was at the limit of the strength I could achieve. No doubt I could learn to control them better and be more accurate, but I couldn't get any more physical power into the vines. *Unless you eat another seed.*

The longer I trained, the more power I wanted. Each time I failed to tug over a heavy target, and each time my vines thudded to a stop instead of powering through whatever they had hit, I ached for more strength. Which was exactly what I was scared of. *Power corrupts. The more you have, the more you want.*

But the difference was, I may need it, rather than just want it. Right now the most important thing for me was to survive the Trials. Zeus and Poseidon both hated me, and they were in charge. Whatever was coming would not be easy. Plus, I couldn't bear the thought of Hades marrying another woman.

Other than a short break for lunch, we only stopped when it was time to get ready for the announcement. I was nervous about my brother, a human who was clearly important to me, being there but Hecate insisted she wouldn't take her eyes off him.

'Don't,' I said sternly. 'Because there are plenty of folk who would try to use him against me.'

'I know, Persy. He'll be fine.' We were back in Hades' rooms, and Sam was completely distracted by Skop, laughing at something so hard his eyes were streaming.

'And will you find him something to wear so that he fits in a bit better?'

'Yes. I will look after him. I promise.'

'Thank you.'

'No worries. He's kinda cute to have around to be honest. He's like you when you get all excited about stuff, except he's better looking. No offense, I'm just not into chicks. I can't wait for him to see a minotaur.' Hecate's eyes were sparkling.

I made a mental note to keep a firm eye on both of them, and Hecate left, telling me she would pick me up again in an hour. I made my way somewhat nervously into the dressing room off Hades' bedroom, not sure what to expect. He had told me that he had kept all my old clothes, and to help myself, but I'd yet to venture in there.

It was a large room with only the one door, and all three other walls were lined with open fronted closets. The closet opposite me was filled with black garments, jeans and shirts and togas, clearly belonging to Hades. But the other two walls were a riot of color and fabric. I took in a breath as I ran my fingers along the rows of dresses, marveling that anyone could own such a huge number of beautiful gowns. Silk, organza, satin, velvet, cotton; every fabric imaginable hung in the closets, and beneath them rows and rows of stunning high-heeled shoes stood shining.

I closed my eyes and spun in a slow circle, deciding that the first dress I laid my hand on would be the one I would wear. I reached out blindly and gripped a soft, lightweight fabric, and opened my eyes. The dress had a high choker collar and no sleeves, and the top half of it was made of intricate ink-black lace, tiny flowers dotting the pattern. The bottom half of the dress was ocean blue, darker at the bottom than the top, and made up of lots of feather-light layers so that it puffed out from the tight lace.

It took me no time to shower in the epic bathroom, I was so excited to get the dress on. And I wasn't disappointed. I found a tall stack of drawers next to the dressing room door which was filled with lacy lingerie and fortunately, given that the lace top half of the dress was see-through, a few practical bras. The dress fitted me like a glove, and I swished and swirled in front of the mirror on the other side of the door, watching my white hair fall against the black lace. I barely recognized myself and it felt good to like what I saw in the mirror. It wasn't just the hair and the clothes. My new confidence ran deeper than that. Heat prickled through me, the bond sparking. I wasn't alone. A god loved me, and I loved him. And somehow that was changing me.

When Hecate came back to collect me, looking fierce in a white PVC corset dress and even more silver jewelry than usual, I felt ready to face the gods and all their guests. Including that douchebag, Zeus. I wanted to know what I would be facing next, nervous anticipation fueling my desire for the Trials to be over.

Sam was wearing a black toga, and even as his sister, I could see that it suited him. He was showing a smattering of chest hair and somehow looked even taller than usual.

'What do you think?' he beamed at me.

'Stay away from anyone Skop tells you to talk to,' I said seriously. 'He's a pervert and a pest.'

'Excellent,' Sam said, rubbing his hands together.

'I mean it, you should stay well away from the gods, Sam. Stick with Hecate.' He gave her a sideways glance, and I saw his eyes dip to the high hem of her skirt.

'Stick with Hecate. Got it,' he said. *Oh no.* Sam having a crush on the celibate goddess of necromancy could not end well.

'Ready to go?' Hecate said, and I nodded. I would have to have a talk with my brother later.

ELEVEN

PERSEPHONE

The announcement was being held in Hades' throne room, and Sam's face when he saw the huge colored flames made me wonder what my own had looked like the first time I was here.

'Geez, Persy, I can't believe this is real,' he breathed as he stared around himself. There were only a few guests already there, but a small group of tall women with skin like tree bark were fawning around an attractive man I recognized from previous meetings as Theseus, and seven or eight minotaur guards ringed the edge of the floating room. I scanned them quickly, looking for Kerato and spotted him by the throne dais.

'Stay here,' I told Sam, and made my way quickly to the Captain of the Guard. 'I'm so pleased to see you, Kerato,' I said as I reached him. He dipped his head low.

'And you, My Lady.'

'Thank you for trying to help me during the last Trial. I'm sorry you were...' I floundered for the right word.

'Killed?' he offered. The stern expression on his snouted face didn't change. 'It is my duty. I will be as strong as I was before in around a hundred years.' I looked at him in shock.

'A hundred years?'

'Yes.'

'Well, that sucks.'

'A hundred years is not a long time, my lady. And Ankhiale is very strong. It could have been worse.'

I considered his words, a weird anticipation buzzing through me. The notion of a hundred years not being a long time threw stark light on the idea of being immortal. I'd known when Hades had told me that we were only married four years how small that amount of time must have seemed to him but... Endless life. Surely there was no point unless you had someone to share it with? The same question I was trying and failing to suppress popped up immediately. *Live without the man you love, or slowly lose your soul with him?*

I shoved the thought away.

'Well, I'm very grateful. You are a credit to Virgo and Hades,' I said to the minotaur, unsure if I was overstepping my role but the words coming anyway. Something flickered in the creature's eyes and when he spoke there was genuine warmth for the first time.

'I should like it if you won the Trials, My Lady.'

'I'll do my best,' I smiled back at him.

. . .

Slowly, more guests arrived, little bursts of light flashing around the room as we sipped from saucer shaped glasses and Sam gaped at everything.

'Can you all transport yourself around like that?' he asked Hecate.

'Nope, only powerful gods can do that. They've all been given an invite that lets them flash here for this event, created by an Olympian.'

'So, how powerful are you?' There was definitely a flirtatious tone to my brother's voice, and to my surprise, Hecate echoed it as she answered him.

'You'll have to wait and find out.'

Oh gods.

'*Is your brother into Hecate?*' asked Skop in my head.

'*If he is, you can be the one to tell him that she's celibate and he can't stay in Olympus,*' I grumbled back.

'Woah, is that Poseidon?' Sam's awed voice drew my attention to where he was pointing, at the dais. Poseidon had shown up with his trident and watery toga, and his blue eyes found mine immediately.

'Yup,' I mumbled. 'And it looks like he still hates me.'

There was a wave of delicious ocean smell, then in a flash I was in a water bubble, the sea god directly in front of me. *Not again*, I groaned internally. I was fed up of being yelled at by gods.

'Hello,' I said tightly, bowing my head.

'I only have a moment before Zeus arrives,' Poseidon said, and I raised my eyebrows in surprise. 'I care more for my brother, Hades, than you may believe, and I see now that he is willing to put our world in danger for you. Rather than fight him, I have decided to help you. With combined strength and foresight, we will be strong enough to avoid any more disasters. We must not have a repeat of the endurance Trial. You must not end up in Tartarus again.'

'Hades told me that I must never meet Cronos,' I said. This time Poseidon looked surprised.

'Good. I am glad you are aware of that. Now, listen to me carefully,' he said, and leaned forward and opened his closed hand. A shining pearl lay in the middle of his palm. 'I have bewitched the hippocampus you bonded with so quickly in my realm.'

'What?' He thrust his hand out to me and I tentatively took the pearl from him. It was warm, and fizzed with energy.

'When you need his help, crush the pearl,' said Poseidon quickly. 'He will appear in the form you most require. But he was not designed to be out of the water for long, so you will only have about five minutes before he must return to Aquarius.'

'Buddy is in the pearl?' My mouth was hanging open as I looked between the sea god and the little gem.

'Yes. Use it wisely,' he said, then the bubble of water around us vanished and he turned to my brother. 'You are foolish to come here, human,' he said to Sam, then strode towards the thrones.

'He's awesome,' breathed Sam. Still too confused to respond, I stared at the pearl. Was Poseidon telling the truth? He had been so fearful and angry before, did he really now believe that he and the others could prevent me from causing any damage if they helped me?

What choice did the sea god have? My racing mind played out his options. If I died, Hades would fall to the monster inside him, then Olympus would be overrun by the dead. If I survived I could be used to release the most evil god in history and start a war. Poseidon was stuck between a rock and a hard place.

But I wasn't sure he knew how close Hades was to succumbing to the dark. Hades had lost me once before and the Underworld had continued on. Did Poseidon know how much stronger the beast inside the King of the Dead had become in my absence?

I eyed the pearl, full of suspicion. Hades said that if I tried to take the power of something primordial in strength I would explode. This tiny pearl could be just that kind of weapon.

'You look incredible.' Hades' voice filtered through my thoughts and I snapped my head up, seeking him out. He was on his throne, his smoky form flickering against the skulls.

'Thanks. You look smoky,' I grinned back at him.

'You know what I like most about that dress?' he asked, his voice a purr.

'No.'

'That I get to take it off later.' Heat washed through me and I felt my cheeks burn. *'Are you blushing?'*

'No! You sound like you've had a good day,' I said, changing the subject.

'For the first time in what feels like centuries, I had

something to look forward to at the end of it,' he said, the playful tone replaced by something much softer. Pleasure at his words made me take a deep breath, my chest swelling.

'*I wish I could kiss you right now,'* I told him.

'*When you are my Queen, you can kiss me whenever the hell you like.'*

'*If that's not a good enough incentive to win, I don't know what is.'*

'That dress looks like my grandmother made it,' a voice sneered from behind me. I turned, expecting to see Eris, the only person I'd met so far who would be so outright rude, but my eyebrows shot up when I saw Minthe instead. As she had been at the masquerade ball, she was dressed in scarlet red, but the dress would have looked more at home in a Manhattan nightclub than at a ball. It was skin tight, with peephole sides showing her toned waist, and a plunging neckline revealing ample cleavage. The skirt was short and she was wearing red boots that came high over her knees. She looked amazing.

My insides quivered as every instinct in me told me to roll-over, to avoid conflict, to let the pretty, popular girl have what she wanted because it would be less trouble for me in the end.

But I wasn't at school anymore, and yes, she might be wearing something more modern than me, but it was my dress Hades wanted to take off.

'Your grandmother must be very talented,' I said, and lifted my glass to my lips nonchalantly.

'Who's this?' said Sam, appearing over my shoulder. I clenched my jaw, annoyed, and lowered the glass.

'This is Minthe,' I ground out.

'I'm Sam,' he beamed, and stuck his hand out.

'You're a human,' she sneered, looking at his hand like it had come out of the Empusa lair.

'And you're rude,' he replied. I snorted a laugh.

'Minthe is the current leader of the Trials,' I told him. 'So not my biggest fan.'

'So you want to win? You're not being forced to compete?' he asked her. She looked at him incredulously.

'Forced to compete? Are you kidding? The Queen of the Underworld is a title most in Olympus would die for. And ironically, when I win I will never die.'

'Minthe is in it for the immortality,' I said to Sam.

'Whereas you're in it for love?' she said, perfect eyebrows raised. 'Spare me the act, Persephone. You've gone from being a pathetic, powerless little human to someone famous across Olympus, with magic. Don't pretend you're not in this for the same reasons as everyone else who's tried.'

'You know nothing about me,' I growled, gripping the stem on my glass tightly. My vines were writhing under my skin. She didn't care one bit for Hades, she would let him rot from the inside out whilst she gloried in being an immortal Queen.

'You're the same as everyone else. There is nothing special about you, despite what people say.'

'You're jealous,' said Sam, and we both looked at him. He gave a her a cold smile. 'You know Hades likes her and she has supporters, and you're jealous.'

I blinked. Nobody was ever jealous of me.

'Shut your mouth or I'll shut it for you,' she snapped at Sam, and the stem of my glass snapped in my grip. I didn't feel the glass cut my hand though, as a black vine snaked from my free hand. Minthe licked her lips slowly as she raised her own hands, the skin on her palms turning an earthy brown.

'Why don't you go and talk to someone else, Minthe?' Hecate appeared from nowhere, stepping between us. Blue light danced over her pale skin and power emanated from her. Minthe stepped backwards, and an angry look flashed over her face, as though she hadn't wanted to move.

'You and your Titan guard-dog are freaks,' she spat, then whirled around, her heels clicking on the marble as she marched away.

'I had that covered, you know,' I said to Hecate, resentfully. I was surprised to feel genuinely robbed of a chance to show Minthe that she shouldn't fuck with me.

'I know you did, but I'm allowed to be a bitch to people. You're not supposed to. This whole thing is being broadcast.'

'Oh,' I said. 'Then, thanks.'

'You're welcome. And you're bleeding.'

I looked down at my hand, the broken glass still clutched in it.

'Shit,' exclaimed Sam, taking the glass from me quickly. 'Is it bad? Let me see.' I smiled at him.

'It's fine. Watch.' I held up my hand to show him, and called up my power, concentrating on the cut. It glowed faintly as the skin closed, and delight spread across Sam's face.

'Now that is fucking cool.'

'Right?'

'You still need to make sure you don't get blood on your dress,' Hecate said, and a satyr tugged at my skirt. He was holding a tray with new drinks and a neatly folded napkin. I thanked him and wiped my hand clean.

'You know, I could get used to living here,' said Sam as the satyr handed him a fresh glass.

'Maybe you should wait until you see the bad stuff before making statements like that,' I said. A loud gong sounded and the commentator shimmered into the room at the same time Zeus appeared on his throne. 'And it doesn't look like you'll have to wait long.'

It was time to find out what my next Trial would be.

TWELVE

HADES

'Good day, Olympus!' boomed the commentator. I tore my eyes from Persephone, her tense anger after her encounter with Minthe rolling through the bond and firing inside me. And despite hating her feeling anything other than happy, I couldn't deny how good it felt knowing how much she resented Minthe. I was hers, and everything about her body and mind projected it and I liked it. In fact I loved it. The idea of being wed to that shallow mountain nymph was too unpleasant to consider.

'It's time to announce the penultimate Trial!' sang the commentator. My stomach tensed in anticipation, magnified by my awareness of Persephone's nerves. 'First thing tomorrow, Persephone will face one of the most exciting and unpleasant demons of the Underworld. One with an appetite for death and destruction.' My pulse quickened. I had known that this Trial would involve one of the nastier demons that inhabited my realm, but there were a few I prayed she would not have to face. A few that I really did not want to have to give up control over for the duration of the Trial, so that Zeus could play his twisted games.

It was impossible for me to guess what demon had been chosen. The depths of Virgo were home to some of the most dangerous creatures ever born, including some the other Olympians didn't even know existed. Many were too dangerous for me to give up control of at all, like the Furies, and some were too strong and willful to be drawn into these games, like Nyx. But Zeus still had a choice of many who would shred a person apart with relish, their power coming from the dead.

The commentator spoke again. 'She will enter the lair of Eurynomos!'

An excited buzz rippled through the crowd as Persephone's eyes snapped to mine, her face paling as my own stomach sank. Eurynomos was the embodied spirit of rotting corpses and one of the worst demons in the Underworld.

Before I could send a word of comfort to Persephone, Zeus stood up.

'See you all tomorrow,' he said, and waved his hand. The room emptied with a flash, and rage seared hot through my veins.

'I have asked you to stop doing that in my realm,' I hissed.

'And I did not agree. You are forbidden from communicating with Persephone before her Trial.'

'What?' I was on my feet, my muscles expanding instinctively. I would not be kept apart from her. Ever again.

'Eurynomos has been under your control for centuries. You will be able to give her an unfair advantage by telling her what you know about him.'

'I will tell her nothing,' I ground out.

'I know. Because you will not be able to.'

'Zeus,' I started, a roaring sound building in my ears and darkness spreading through my core. He would not keep me from her.

'Hades, it is for one night, and you can't deny that your information would help her. It is what is fair,' said Athena, standing up. 'She will be told, and kept safe.'

'Nobody can keep her safe except me.'

'Untrue,' said Zeus, but Athena cut him off.

'She's not going anywhere, you can guard her bedroom door if you wish. You just can't speak to her.'

The rational part of me warred with the shadowed fury. If they were all in agreement I couldn't do anything about it. This was a battle I couldn't win. But perhaps I could get something from it.

'I will agree on one condition,' I spat.

'You don't have a choice,' drawled Zeus, but Athena cocked her head at me.

'And what is that?'

'Leave her brother out of the Trials. He is to remain untouched.' Zeus rolled his eyes but Athena spoke.

'And you will not try to talk to her if we agree?'

'Yes.'

'Fine.'

'You spoil him, daughter,' Zeus said to Athena, then disappeared with a screech of purple lightning. She looked at me, her face soft.

'You are lucky that I'm his favorite,' she said with a small smile, then vanished too. As the other gods began to leave, their thrones vanished as well, the dais reforming with just my huge skull throne in the middle. I strode towards it, still hulking and angry.

Zeus would pay for what he done to her. *To us.* I wasn't sure how yet, but he would.

'A word, if I may, Hades?' Poseidon strode up to my throne, and I nodded, surprise knocking my anger back a little.

'What do you want?'

'Brother, I am worried. Someone sent Persephone to Tartarus deliberately, and very few know the true consequences of that.'

'If you are going to ask me to send her back again, I won't.'

'On the contrary. I have decided she is safer where we can see and control her.'

'Control her?' Alarm bells rang in my mind, a need to protect her flaring inside me.

'You know what I mean,' he said dismissively. 'I believe that the culprit is closer to home than we originally thought.'

'You think it is an Olympian,' I said sharply. It wasn't a question.

'Yes. And since you are clearly still in love with her, you are the only one I can rule out. Hence this conversation.'

'Who do you suspect?' If the sea god was in the mood to talk, then I should get what I could out of him, and revisit the statement about controlling Persephone later.

'Ares has not had a war in a while, Hera has wrath more lethal than any of us, Aphrodite's boredom knows no bounds, Athena makes wild plans beyond any of our understanding and Dionysus has been acting strange for weeks.'

'And Zeus?'

'He has the most to lose.'

'Or the most to prove,' I countered. 'And the most hatred for me.'

'He does not hate you, brother.'

'Really? So forcing me to marry against my will and exposing my realm to the world is an act of love?' My voice dripped with sarcasm.

'When Olympus discovers that it was you who created a new realm against Zeus' will, and that the Lord of the Gods can't undo it, they will lose respect for him. You know he can not tolerate that. You have brought this upon yourself.'

I hissed out a breath, unable to argue. A thought flashed into my mind.

'Oceanus may have a score to settle,' I said. Poseidon scowled.

'Oceanus is your friend and my mentor. I do not believe this would be in his interest.'

'You are right,' I said, feeling guilty for suggesting it. Oceanus was a Titan, and easily powerful enough to be the culprit, but he had never been malevolent. And I knew better than most not to judge Titans by their few monstrous ancestors. 'If Zeus has the most to lose, then could it be someone with a vendetta against him, rather than Persephone?' I said.

'That moves Hera to the top of the list,' Poseidon muttered. 'I'll never know why she married him.'

'He's as charming as he is fickle. How do I know it is not you, and this is not an elaborate scheme to dissuade me of your guilt?' I said, glaring into Poseidon's ocean-blue eyes. He chuckled softly.

'Brother, I certainly mean you no harm. It is true I fear what your lover could do to Olympus, but I am not so governed by pride that I will let my initial reaction stand. I want to help her win, for something in return.'

'What?'

'If she survives and she wins the Trials and gets her power back, let her live elsewhere.'

Anger trickled through my veins like ice.

'No,' I said immediately. Poseidon's face darkened, waves crashing in his irises.

'Hades, she can not stay so close to Tartarus and you know it. The more her soul deteriorates, the less control you or anyone else will have over her.'

'I do not seek to control her!'

'Do you mean to let the most powerful and evil being

Olympus has ever seen go free?'

'Of course not but-' He cut me off before I could finish.

'Then make the right choice, Hades. She would be happier anywhere but here.'

The sick feeling in my gut spread, the knowledge that he was right worse than the anger roiling inside me.

'She can survive the Trials without your help,' I spat eventually.

'You are making a mistake.'

'This conversation is over.'

He gave me a long look, then the salty smell of ocean washed over me as he gave a bark of frustration and vanished. I closed my eyes, searching inside me for the remnants of Persephone's light, the barrier she had helped reinforce with her golden vines. I filled my head and my heart with her, and slowly the monster receded, sinking back into its toxic depths.

She had beaten many Trials already that should have killed her. There were only two left now, and then this nightmare would be over, one way or another.

But no matter how I spun it in my mind, I couldn't see a happy ending. If she died... The thought of losing her was unbearable, and I cast it out before the beast could rise again. If she survived but lost the Trials, I could not marry that nymph. And if she triumphed... Could I really let her give up her soul to live with me in the dark?

THIRTEEN

PERSEPHONE

'What do you mean I can't see Hades?'

'It has been deemed that he would be able to give you an unfair advantage,' Athena said, her voice serene as she stood before me in my old room.

'I deserve an advantage!' I snapped. 'This is bullshit.' Power burst from the goddess and my knee buckled instantly, forcing me into a bow.

'Do not forget who you are addressing, Persephone.'

'I'm sorry,' I stammered, my heart hammering in my chest.

'Standing up to Zeus as you did wasn't just brave, it was stupid. Under any other circumstance he would have killed you where you stood. Do not think you can treat all gods in that way.' Her voice held a steely edge and I tried to lift my head to look at her.

'I am still learning your customs,' I said. *Plus Zeus was an asshole who deserved what I had said to him.* Athena regarded me a moment, then gave a tiny nod. My body relaxed, and I stood up again. 'Can I see Hecate and my brother?'

'No. Hecate knows as much about the inhabitants of this realm as Hades does.' I barely kept the scowl from my face. At least I had Skop, I thought, glancing down at the silent dog. 'Rest well in preparation for tomorrow,' Athena said.

'I don't suppose you can tell me anything? About what to expect?' I ventured.

'No. I can't. Goodnight, Persephone.'

The goddess of wisdom vanished before I could say anything else and I sighed as I slumped onto my bed. It felt small now, compared to Hades' bed. A flash of anger and regret pulsed through me as I remembered his words from earlier, about having something to look forward to all day. And now we were being denied each other's company.

'They're all assholes,' I said, kicking out at thin air.

'*Dionysus is alright,*' said Skop.

'You would say that, you work for him.'

'*Doesn't mean I have to like him. I just do.*'

'So he's not cruel or spiteful or egotistical?' I challenged. Skop snorted.

'*He's all of those things. You can't have almost limitless power and endless life, and not think you're better than everyone else. Or become a bit fucked up along the way.*'

'So why do you like him then?'

'*Because the good outweighs the bad. Plus, your definition of bad is a little different to mine.*' He wagged his tail.

'I don't doubt it,' I said wryly and stood up, my feet pacing automatically.

Nerves were making my skin fizz, and the thought of waiting until tomorrow for the Trial with no Hades to distract me was making me even more anxious. 'Do you know anything about Eurynomos?' I asked Skop.

'*Only what Hecate told you, that he's the demon of rotting corpses.*'

'Shit. I hoped I had mis-remembered that,' I said, pushing my hands through my hair. 'Maybe I should practice that thing I did in the Empusa lair where I blocked out the bad smell.'

'*Good idea. Rotting-corpse smell could be quite distracting.*' My stomach lurched, a combination of revulsion at the visual my brain conjured up, and my building nerves. '*You know what would be even more useful than practicing smell-blocking?*' Skop said, and I looked at the little dog, raising my eyebrows in question.

'What?'

'*Eating another seed and getting more magic.*'

I paused my pacing.

I knew he was right. There were two Trials left, and they were only going to get harder. Was the risk of more power corrupting me greater than the risk of dying? Survival instinct took over, the urge to make myself stronger filling me. *You're not just risking dying*, my internal voice reminded me. *If you survive but lose, you have to watch Hades marry Minthe.*

I had to win.

I stepped to my dresser, where the box of seeds stood. It magically appeared in whatever place I was staying, along with *Faesforos* and the old purse I had arrived in Olympus with. Flipping open the lid of the box, I took a slow breath.

Just a little more power. Enough to beat Eurynomos, and take on the last Trial.

And possibly find the river Lethe, like the stranger in the Atlas garden had said. I shoved the thought down. I had to concentrate on the Trials.

I picked up a shiny, moist seed. What would more magic feel like? Just more strength? Or would there be new powers?

I put the seed in my mouth and swallowed.

Unlike the previous times I had eaten a seed, I did feel something right away but it was not what I had hoped for. It was massive fatigue. Within a few minutes I felt the need to lay down, my eyelids leaden, and almost as soon as my head hit the pillow I was out, my sleep completely dreamless.

I woke with a start the next morning when Skop picked up my hand in his wet mouth and shook it.

'What happened?' I shouted, sitting up quickly.

'You slept like the freaking dead and I had to stay up all night to check you were breathing,' he answered me, my hand still in his mouth. I tugged it back gently.

'Well, thanks,' I mumbled, blinking.

'How do you feel?'

'Good,' I said, swinging my legs out of bed. And it was true. My mind felt clearer and my nerves, though still present, weren't as overwhelming as before. Maybe being knocked out like that was exactly what I had needed. I'd had no chance to freak myself out. 'How long until the Trial?'

'An hour.'

'OK. I'm going for a shower,' I said, and made my way to my washroom.

Whilst I washed up and got ready, I did what I had meant to do the night before, practicing blocking out the smell of the soap by thinking about the smell of plants instead. Lavender definitely worked the best, which made sense as it was such a potent smell. I whipped out my vines a few times, checking the color and testing how they felt. Other than a keener sense of alertness, everything felt the same.

Dressed in my fighting gear, *Faesforos* strapped to my thigh, Poseidon's pearl in my pocket and my hair tightly braided out of my face, I felt more ready than I ever had before a Trial. I could kill demons. I was a goddess, dammit.

And I had one hell of a god to fight for.

When it wasn't Hecate who came to get me I felt a pang of nerves though. Athena returned instead, her white toga pristine. I hadn't realized how much confidence the fierce goddess of ghosts instilled in me until she wasn't there, and I missed her.

'You are different,' Athena said, tilting her head at me as soon as she appeared in my room. I bowed low as I answered her. I didn't want to piss her off again.

'I ate another seed.'

'That was probably wise.'

'Coming from you, I'll take that reassuringly,' I muttered as I straightened and she gave me a small smile.

'Are you ready?'

I nodded.

She flashed us to a cavern that glowed the same dim red that the Empusa's lair had, but it was much bigger. I turned slowly, looking around. It was completely empty, just bare rock everywhere.

'Good luck,' Athena said quietly, then vanished with a flash. The commentator's voice rang out immediately, and I felt a shot of adrenaline rush through me, my stomach lurching. This was it.

'Good day, Olympus! As you can see, Persephone is ready to start her next Trial, in the lair of Eurynomos!' I moved my hand to my side, nearer to my dagger. This didn't look like a lair. Where were the corpses and stuff? 'But let us not forget, good citizens, this is the penultimate Trial. We need some drama!'

My jaw clenched. Was me fighting a horrendous demon not enough for these fucking people?

'Persephone will be offered a choice. A test of her moral character.' I froze as the new voice boomed around me.

It was Zeus speaking.

'There is no catch or hidden agenda, and it is a rare opportunity indeed.' His seductive voice bounced off the bare cave walls and adrenaline surged through me. *Get on with it!*

Purple light began to crackle above me and I stared up at the ceiling of the cavern as something began to melt through it, entering the space.

Not something. Someone.

A woman's form began to take shape, emerging from the rock, facing down towards the ground as though she were laying on her front. She was wearing a red dress which hung from her suspended body, and she looked to be bound by ropes. Her hair also hung down, obscuring her face from view.

But I knew who it was without seeing her face.

'Get me the fuck out of here!' screeched Minthe.

'Persephone,' Zeus's voice boomed. 'We would like you to meet Eurynomos, demon of rotting flesh.' The walls rippled with red light, and shadows began forming on the flat walls where there shouldn't be any. I gripped my dagger instinctively, my vines itching at my palms. A whimper drew my attention back to Minthe, held against the ceiling by ropes forming a sort of net. Blackened fingers were snaking between the ropes from the rock, drawing closer to her.

'He is usually only able to take the flesh from the dead, but we've made an exception for today,' Zeus said, and Minthe screamed as a finger touched her bare shoulder. Her pale skin darkened instantly, as though she had been burned.

'Stop!' I yelled. 'This is my Trial, not hers!'

'So true, flower goddess. You need two more seeds to win. You may have both, right now, if you let Eurynomos have Minthe.'

'What?' My head spun at his words. I could win right now? No more tests and Trials and fear, just Hades.

But...

I looked up at the woman strapped to the ceiling, a flash of memory causing me to think of Ixion strapped to the burning wheel in Tartarus. My stomach lurched as another finger touched Minthe's leg, and she made a strangled sound.

'This isn't fair!' she screamed. 'I've taken my Trials! I've proven myself!'

She was right.

'If you choose to save her and succeed you will win one token, and therefore will need to win the last Trial to marry Hades,' boomed Zeus. 'If you choose to save her and fail, you lose the Trials. What is it to be, Persephone?'

There was no question in my mind. Maybe the fucked up gods and citizens of Olympus would kill for what they wanted, but I wasn't one of them. I couldn't live my life waking every day knowing I chose to let someone die.

'Let her live,' I said loudly.

'I was hoping you would say that,' Zeus said, and I could hear the delight in his words. The cavern began to rumble and shake around me, and I yelped as a huge part of the rock floor began to crack and split, causing me to stumble.

'*I was hoping you would say that too,*' hissed a high-pitched voice inside my head. '*It's so rare that I get living company, it is truly a treat.*'

'Eurynomos?' I called out loud, as more of the floor cracked around me.

'*Indeed. Now, if you want to save her you must cut her free.*'

I looked up at Minthe strapped to the ceiling. How was I going to get up there?

With a lurch, the part of the floor I was standing on shot up, and I dropped to my knees as I stumbled. The floor was falling away in huge pieces, leaving pillars of stone at different heights, barely large enough for me to stand on. The one I was on was one of the lowest, but some almost reached the ceiling. As I stared around I realized what I had to do. I had to jump from pillar to pillar, until I was high enough to cut Minthe's ropes.

Heights. Why was it fucking heights! They said I wouldn't have to face them again.

I peered over the edge of my pillar, pulse racing and heart hammering so hard I felt sick.

But the dark chasm I expected to see wasn't there. What I saw was much, much worse.

Bodies. Corpses in every stage of decomposition were rising from the dark, filling the space between the pillars. Many were skeletons like the one I had fought at the start of the Trials, limbs and jaws clacking as they climbed over each other. But some still had flesh clinging to their bones, jaws and shoulders and ribs showing through their sallow, blue-tinged skin. I felt myself heave as their rotten smell rose with them, and called the lavender scent to wrap around me fast.

'Don't fall off the pillars, flower goddess,' taunted Eurynomos. *'They'll rip you apart, and then I'll eat your flesh.'*

Shit, shit, shit. Terror surged inside me as I looked between the writhing mass of undead below me, and Minthe, shrieking above me. How the fuck was I going to survive this?

FOURTEEN

PERSEPHONE

OK, *human Persephone was scared of heights,* I told myself sternly, breathing hard. *Goddess Persephone has vines that can catch stuff and recently jumped out of a tree. Goddess Persephone can do this.*

'Will you get the fuck on with it!' screamed Minthe from above me. I flicked my eyes to her angrily as I tried to work out which rocky pillar was closest to me.

'Are you shitting me? I could have left you here to die!'

'Well you didn't, so get me the fuck out of here!'

'Stop swearing at me and shut up,' I snapped back, tucking *Faesforos* back into its sheath. A low rumbling moan was coming from the undead below me, and I guessed some must still have their throats intact. I let a green vine snake from my palm, aiming it towards the ceiling. The closest pillar was about a foot taller than the one I was on and a three feet leap away. I felt a thud beneath me, and my stomach lurched as a rotten hand appeared over the edge of my pillar. The undead were climbing.

My lip curled back as I kicked out at the hand, and I watched in muted fear as the corpse fell back onto the mass of skeletons below it. Another corpse replaced it immediately.

Minthe was right. I needed to get the fuck on with it.

My vine wrapped itself around the ropes holding Minthe up, and I tugged experimentally. The vine held firm. So I could jump, and the vine should hold me if I missed. Like a safety rope. A safety rope over corpses that would tear me apart before my flesh was eaten.

My hands were shaking as I bent my knees and gripped the vine, preparing to jump. Just a few weeks ago my knees would have given out already, but I was different now. I was strong. And I had to win. Filling my mind with Hades' face, I jumped.

I landed easily on the next pillar, the vine helping me get the height I needed, and a cry of triumph escaped my lips.

'There's like ten more! Gods help me, stop celebrating and hurry up!' shouted Minthe. I threw her a glare, and found the next easiest pillar to get to. They seemed to be in no order, but there was one about four feet away that was higher than mine. I felt the rock pound beneath me, and didn't need to look down to know that it meant the undead were still trying to get to me.

'Did you know that's how Spartae Skeletons were

made?' Eurynomos' hissing voice filled my head. *'They are what's left when I've finished with the flesh.'*

'Lovely', I muttered, crouching for the next jump.

'Hades lets me have the bad ones, you see. The ones who have sinned most foully.'

'That's nice,' I replied, and jumped. I didn't land so easily this time, the pillar higher and further than before, and my insides lurched as my back foot scrabbled on the edge of the rock.

'I don't miss him, you know. Hades never lets me have any fun, and I'm bound to his will. This Zeus character who controls me now though...' The demon tailed off and I couldn't help my interest.

'What about him?'

'He doesn't have what it takes,' Eurynomos hissed. *'He has power, but it's not dark enough to contain me. Not for much longer anyway.'*

A shudder ran through me at his words. Could he really break free of Zeus' power?

'Hades would just take control again,' I said flippantly, and decided on my next pillar. It was only a couple of feet away, but it was much higher than mine. A bony finger crept over the edge of my own pillar as I bent my knees, and I kicked at it. Eurynomos sighed loudly in my head.

'Yes, he would. But I might get a few brief seconds of blissful freedom first,' he said more brightly.

'And what would you do with that?' I leaped for the next pillar, and realized with a jolt that I wouldn't make it. Instinct took over and my vines shortened fast. Too fast. I flew up and over the pillar, dangling from my vine, the sense of weightlessness nauseating. I couldn't help looking down as I swung and black dots instantly clouded my eyes. Swarms of undead surged between the uneven pillars below me, and the thought of falling to them was the only thing I could process.

'Just pull yourself up, you idiot!' shouted Minthe. Her voice cut through my panic, and I did as she said, shortening the vine further. I began to zoom upwards, and I kicked myself mentally. *Why the hell didn't I do this before?*

'Oh no, no, it can't be this easy,' hissed Eurynomos, and then searing heat flashed down my vine towards me. One of the blackened fingers on the ceiling that had been tormenting Minthe was gripping my vine, burning through it. Revolting images of the decomposing dead flashed through me as my vines turned black, the dark power of the Underworld filling me.

And then I really was weightless, the vine severed by the demon's touch. I whipped a new vine from my other hand out blindly, praying as I twisted through the air, all other thought gone. It hit something hard and I willed it to coil around whatever it was. I jerked, and then I was swinging towards a tall pillar, my vine wrapped tight around the top, and bony fingers were closing around my ankle. I kicked at the skeleton as I looked down, my insides lurching again as a squelchy, rotten fist gripped my boot. I smashed into the pillar hard, the momentum of my fall enough to jolt the undead's grip loose, and then I willed the vine to shorten, shooting me up to the top of the pillar and out of reach. I was panting hard when I got to the top, and I scrabbled up onto the rock, adrenaline making my muscles stronger.

Minthe screamed again, and the undead moaned louder in response. I needed to end this. But how, if Eurynomos was going to sever my vines? They were all I had. Maybe I could distract him.

'Where are you, Eurynomos? Why don't you show yourself?' I yelled. He chuckled in my mind.

'That is forbidden.'

'Are you too ugly to be seen then?' I eyed the next pillar and instead of sending my vines up to the ropes, I launched them from both hands at the top of it. It took more physical effort to climb the pillars like this than swinging from the ceiling, but at least the fingers couldn't get me. I pulled myself to the next pillar using the vines, and bashed my chin on it hard as I collided with the rock, my feet scrabbling for purchase. I dragged myself onto the top, scanning fast for the next one.

'You might call me ugly I suppose,' the demon said thoughtfully. I launched my vines at the next pillar. I reckoned I had another three or four to go, before I could reach the ceiling. I glanced up at Minthe, and saw that her eyes were squeezed shut. Now I was closer I could see the gaping wounds the fingers were leaving, burning through layers of skin. Bile burned in my chest. I had to get us both out. I jumped, trying to pull on the vines earlier so that I didn't hit the pillar so hard. It didn't work, and my shoulder took a pounding as I slammed into the next pillar.

'*What do you think?*' said Eurynomos' voice as I pulled myself up. I scowled through my panting.

'What do I think of what?'

'*Am I ugly?*'

Just as I straightened on top of the spindly pillar, he appeared, right in front of me.

My brain froze as I stumbled backwards in primal fright, and the only part of me to react to my feet slipping off the rock were my vines. They whipped towards the only thing to grab; Eurynomos.

His face twisted in delight as my vines made contact with his skin, and although my fall was halted, images so revolting I almost passed out flooded my mind. I could see him, on all fours, surrounded by corpses. His body was black and hairless, long and sinewy, and covered in sores that oozed dark red liquid that streaked his skin. Massive black eyes bulged in his elongated skull and his mouth was far too big, filled with razor-sharp, crooked teeth. The real demon, cackling before me, merged with the one in my vision, who was ripping flesh from bodies with his teeth like a rabid animal.

'You smell delicious,' he hissed, and I convulsed as I forced my vines to let go, to disintegrate. With another roar of laughter he vanished. '*Such a shame I'm not allowed to touch you until you fail to save the other one,*' he said, his voice mockingly sad. I was taking deep breaths, trying desperately not to throw up or pass out, my knees weak beneath me on the pillar.

'Get the fuck on with it, flower girl!' yelled Minthe. Anger surged through me at her words.

'I'm nearly killing myself to save you, you ungrateful asshole!' I yelled back. Weirdly the words brought strength though, and I realized my anger was pushing through the disgust and fear. My shaking lessened and I looked up.

I had to try something else.

I pulled *Faesforos* from my thigh and launched a vine at the ropes above me, near to Minthe's head. It curled around the rope and with a thought, the vine began to shorten, pulling me towards the ceiling fast. I knew I only had seconds before the fingers severed my vine, but hopefully that would be enough. As soon as I got close enough I slashed with my dagger. *Faesforos* cut through the rope like it was butter, and Minthe yelped as her right shoulder dropped.

'What happens if you manage to cut them all?'

'You'd better hope we get flashed out of here before you land in that,' I answered her, pointing at the undead clamoring below us, just as a finger closed over my vine. I winced but stayed focused, looking for a pillar to land on safely. I swung myself, adrenaline edging out the fear, the knowledge that I'd fallen from here already and survived giving me the strength I needed. When I judged I was swinging enough, I lengthened the vine again, kicking my feet towards the highest pillar and letting out a gasp of relief as my feet made contact and I was able to disintegrate the vine. The hideous images crawling from those blackened fingers were impossible to ignore.

'*Clever flower goddess,*' hissed Eurynomos. I ignored him, looking up at the ropes instead and preparing to repeat the maneuver.

Each time I swung from the ceiling I was able to cut more ropes, despite the rotten fingers getting faster at trying to sever my vines. And each time I did it, the stronger and more confident I became. The old saying 'what doesn't kill you makes you stronger,' clearly had some truth to it. After six swings there was only one rope left, and Minthe's face was a mask of fear. Her shoulders and shins were covered in wounds.

'You'd better not fuck this up,' she called to me as I prepared to swing again.

'Have you always been a bitch?' I yelled back.

'Yes. But I don't deserve to die like this.' Her voice was bitter and I couldn't help the surge of emotion I felt for her. She was a fighter, that much was clear, and she had been rendered helpless. I knew how awful it felt to have your fate in the hands of another.

'Perhaps you could be less of a bitch to me if I save your life?' She didn't answer, but her eyes locked on mine and I could see the very real fear under the attitude. 'Alright, I'm coming,' I breathed, and launched my vine up. Weirdly though, as I pulled myself to the ceiling, no finger appeared in the rock, snaking towards my vine. Suspicion filled me as I swiped *Faesforos* at the last rope, which was wrapped around Minthe's middle.

But it never made contact. Instead, Eurynomos appeared between us, my dagger tearing across his emaciated arm. He shrieked, a hair-raising noise that

induced almost as much terror in me as one of Hades'
rages.

'Pain!' the demon screeched, and I kicked at the air
under me, trying to swing myself away from him. I looked
desperately for a pillar beneath me to land on. 'Pain was
what I needed! For a surge in power big enough to break
free!'

'What?' I snapped my eyes to his warped, glee-filled
ones.

'Free,' he hissed, and then he was on me.

Agony like I had never experienced, worse than being
electrocuted by the man with the phoenix, engulfed me. I
could feel my skin being torn from my bones as he bent
his head to my shoulder, and I felt my vine disintegrate as
I screamed. I began to fall, and the demon fell with me,
my neck and my jaw searing with white hot pain as his
teeth sank into my flesh. As darkness began to consume
me, I heard Minthe.

'Fucking fight him!'

My back hit something hard, and I was vaguely
aware of the clatter of bones and the squelch of rotting
flesh. *You are a goddess.* Another wave of agony drew new
screams from me, and I was drowning under Eurynomos'
weight as he tore more skin and muscle from my neck.
You are a goddess. Fucking fight him. I reached inside for
everything I had and blasted my black vines at him.

They hit the demon so hard they went *through* him.
I surged all the power I had through my palms, the

black vines drawing on his foul magic and channeling it as my own strength. Eurynomos bellowed as huge thorned barbs appeared on the vines, and through the connection my vines had to him, I felt them pierce the inside of his chest. As the vines grew they dragged him up, and I swung my arms, slamming him into the side of the cavern. The swarm of undead around me froze in place, only moving their heads to watch their master as I threw him into the opposite wall with as much force as I could muster. I drew my knees up, a dark rage fueled by the demon's power beginning to consume me. *Eurynomos would die.* He and all the others who sought to use me as a toy, torture me for entertainment, rip the fucking flesh from my bones. I was too entrenched in rage to notice that my skin was already knitting back together.

'Get me out of here!' Minthe's shrieks filtered through the toxic rage, and I stood slowly, my eyes still fixed on Eurynomos as I flung him between the cavern walls, his languid body bending unnaturally every time he hit the rock.

'One minute,' I hissed. 'I have something to take care of first.'

With my arms raised high above my head, the black vines glistening with the demon's blood, I held Eurynomos still above me. 'Tell me again how you are going to feast on my flesh?' I yelled at him. My voice didn't sound like my own, but I didn't care.

I didn't care about anything other than making an example of this evil creature. He moaned but didn't reply.

Couldn't reply. I was drawing too much of his power from him.

With a final effort of will I tugged on the darkest part of him, drawing the magic into myself, and then with a roar I swelled my vines with it. Eurynomos screamed as giant thorns erupted from the vines, through his chest, skewering him from the inside out.

As the creature's life left him, so did the dark power flowing into me, and I stumbled backwards as my vines weakened. Eurynomos' body crashed towards the floor and the undead parted as he landed hard in front of me, staring down at his pierced and bloody body. He began to glow a deep blue, then vanished. My black vines disintegrated and an epic wave of nausea took me. Before I could do anything else I was heaving, throwing up onto the rock floor, my body shaking uncontrollably.

'Get me out, please.' Minthe's pleading cut through my retching.

The acrid bile and the pain in my throat and neck made my eyes water as I tried to take deep breaths. *I had to get us out of here.* I shot a green vine towards the ceiling and my exhausted, shaken body didn't even register the height as I pulled myself up, grabbing *Faesforos* from my thigh as I went. I felt dazed, numb. Avoiding meeting Minthe's eyes, I cut the last rope binding her, and the cavern flashed white.

FIFTEEN

PERSEPHONE

A smattering of clapping met my ringing ears as I found myself standing in Hades' throne room.

'Persephone,' his voice filled my head immediately. *'Are you alright?'*

I nodded mutely at the vibrating smoky figure at the end of the row of thrones.

'Persephone!' I whirled at the bellowed voice and saw my brother trying to push his way through the small crowd, frantic. Hecate was yanking him back, her face set and hard.

'I'm fine, Sam,' I croaked, and he stilled, face pale. The burbling sound my voice made wasn't right, and I tentatively touched my neck. My stomach roiled as my fingers didn't meet skin, but something lumpy and wet. I closed my eyes and concentrated, willing the wound to heal faster than it already was. I had no doubt it had been worse when Eurynomos first attacked me, or I wouldn't be still be standing. I'd be dead.

'Alright for some,' muttered Minthe and I opened my eyes. She was standing next to me, shaking. Deep dark burn wounds covered her body, and her face was as white as a sheet. I frowned at her.

'What do you mean, alright for some? You think that was fun for me? That I'm lucky I got to experience that? I just saved your life, quit giving me shit.'

'I meant that,' she said quietly, and gestured to my shoulder and neck, 'I can't heal myself.'

'Oh,' I said. I cocked my head at her, then sent out a vine slowly towards her arm. She flinched when it touched, but said nothing as my vine turned gold, and I sent my healing power through it. Her lips parted in a small gasp, then the sores began to pale, then knit closed.

'Thanks,' she mumbled.

'I'm thrilled to see you two getting on,' boomed Zeus, rising from his throne with a cold smile. 'If you please,' he said and raised his arm. The commentator appeared with a pop.

'So, gutsy Persephone chose to save her rival instead of living with murder on her conscience! Let's see what the judges have to say about that!' He grinned. The judges fizzled into the space in front of the thrones.

'Radamanthus?'

'One token,' the judge said.

'Aeacus?'

'One token.' The gaunt judge eyed me suspiciously as he spoke.

'Minos?'

'One token. And my respect,' said the head judge,

with a small smile. I raised my eyebrows in surprise, and the three of them vanished.

'As I'd hoped, it appears that we will have quite a showdown for the last Trial,' said Zeus loudly.

'How did you know I wouldn't take both tokens and end it there?' I asked, interrupting him. He glared at me.

'Because most humans are painfully predictable, you even more so,' he said, then looked back to the crowd. 'The last Trial will be the much anticipated Hell-Hound Run!' A huge cheer went up from behind me and I looked to Hades. Skop had said I would meet Cerberus at some point. I guess this would be it. 'The Trial will be a little different than it has been for the other contestants though. Previously, the goal has been to get past all three of Hades' pets in a chariot. This time, it will be a race between the last remaining competitors. The winner will marry Hades.'

I looked at Minthe, her jaw dropping in time with mine.

'But I've already survived the Hell-Hound Run, you can't make me do it again!' she protested, her voice aghast. Abruptly she seemed to realize what she'd said and dropped fast to one knee. 'Oh Zeus, I'm sorry, I am just shocked. Please forgive my outburst.'

'You shall both be allowed a team of two to ride the chariot with you. They may not be Olympians, but that is the only restriction,' Zeus continued, ignoring her completely. 'We start at midday tomorrow.' He clapped his hands together in an overly exaggerated gesture, and all the gods except Hades disappeared in a blinding flash.

'Shit!' shouted Minthe, stamping her foot as she straightened. My vine fell away from her.

'What happens in the Hell-Hound Run?' I asked her, aware that Hades was moving towards us on one side, my brother and Hecate on the other.

'As if I'd tell you,' she snarled, fixing her angry eyes on mine.

'Woah, don't blame me for this! Honestly, you are the most ungrateful person I've ever fucking met!' Anger swelled through me.

'You have no idea what's at stake for me. What I've given up for this.' Tears shone in her eyes.

'No, and I don't care! You want to use Hades for immortality, you won't make him happy.'

'Happy? You seriously think you can make the Lord of the Dead *happy*?' She gaped at me.

'I know I can.'

'Wow. You're more deluded than I thought you were.'

'And you're more of a bitch than I thought you were.' Dark smoke entered my peripheral vision and we both looked at Hades.

'Please send me home to prepare, My Lord,' said Minthe tightly, bowing her head. Hades flicked a smoke hand, and she vanished.

'Persy, what the fuck was that? I mean, you were badass, but I can't believe you really did that, my own sister-' My brother's words faded into noise as he barreled into me, wrapping his arms around me hard. My head was buzzing, the residual rage and shock of what I'd done to Eurynomos settling over me.

I should regret such an act of rage. I didn't have to kill Eurynomos. I could have left him trapped while I freed Minthe. But I had decided he would die, and nothing could have stopped me doing it. It had been an act of wrath. The thing I feared most about this other person, this goddess, inside of me.

But I didn't regret it at all. He was not a person, he was a demon. And that meant...

'He'll regenerate,' I said to Hades. I didn't phrase it as a question but as something I'd known before I'd killed him, a defense of my actions. But I needed to hear him confirm it.

Hades nodded.

'Yes. It may take a while, but yes.' A shudder of relief rocked through me. I wasn't a murderer.

'Persy, Slayer of Demons,' said Hecate, a smile on her face. 'I like that.'

'I could get used to it,' I grinned back. My grin slipped as I felt a surge of emotion through me that was not my own. Fear and desperation. *Hades*.

'I need a moment with Hades,' I said to Sam, extracting myself from his hug. 'Then we'll prepare for the next Trial and have a drink. A large one.'

'I'll get the cocktails ready,' said Hecate.

'What's wrong?' I asked as soon as the throne room was empty. The smoke surrounding him fell away and Hades rushed at me. He scooped me up in his huge arms, planting soothing kisses across my neck and shoulder, where Eurynomos had bitten me.

'If you hadn't killed him, I would have,' he whispered, pulling away and gripping my face in his hands. 'You were... incredible.'

'I wouldn't have killed him if he were a real person,' I said firmly. *You sure about that?* The voice inside me came from nowhere, and I forced it down. I was sure. 'I ate another seed,' I told Hades.

'I can see that. The thorns are back.'

'What else can I do now?'

'Heal yourself faster,' he said, silver eyes flicking to my neck. 'I wish I could stay with you, but I have to meet with the other gods, and it can't wait.' I felt his fury rise within him, and laid my palms on his chest. He took a deep breath. 'Zeus lost control of Eurynomos. I do not want to risk him losing control of Cerberus.'

'Will Cerberus try to eat me?' I asked, as casually as I could. Hades stroked his thumb down my cheek.

'He loved you once.'

'Really? I'm more of a cat person.'

'If you become my Queen again, we can get a cat.' My reaction must have shown on my face because a broad smile spread over his.

'You swear?'

'I swear.'

'Watch me ace this Trial,' I said.

After kissing me like his life depended on it, Hades left to meet with the others gods, promising to tell me all about the hell-hounds when he returned. And show me whatever my gold vines were able to do now.

He flashed me back to my old rooms, where Hecate, Sam and Skop were waiting, with the promised cocktails.

'We can only have a quick celebratory drink now, as we have a dinner invitation,' said Hecate, passing me a glass.

'I still can't believe you killed that thing, Persy, honestly, it was crazy!' Sam interrupted. 'And your neck... I thought you were going to die at one point.' He stopped speaking abruptly, a haunted look taking over his face.

'I'm OK, Sam. A demon is no match for a goddess.' I squeezed his arm encouragingly and took a long drag of my drink. It tasted divine.

'Well yeah, you proved that! You didn't tell me about the thorns.'

'I didn't have them until this morning. I ate another seed.'

'Good,' said Hecate. 'That might have saved your life.'

'*Told ya,*' said Skop.

'*And you were right,*' I answered him with a reluctant nod, then turned to Hecate. 'Who is the dinner invitation from?' *Please not Zeus, please not Zeus,* I prayed silently.

'Morpheus and Hedone. And I think they have good news.'

Hecate flashed us to Morpheus' rooms as soon I'd gulped down my cocktail, and boy did I get some room-envy.

His rooms were just like him, ethereal and floaty and just... magical. There was no better word. The rock walls glowed with stars but of every shade of blue, and they seemed to move like liquid across the rock. Just like his flowy robes. An enormous dining table was laid for five in the middle of the reception room and in the center was a large orb that glowed with yellow light, reminding me of the sun and casting a softer atmosphere across the whole space. Bookcases lined one wall, and an enormous tapestry covered the other. Before I could inspect it though, both Hedone and Morpheus were rising from the table to greet us.

'Persy, you were brilliant today!' beamed Hedone, kissing both of my cheeks. Familiar heat flushed through me at her touch and I felt a pang of sympathy for my brother. He would be completely bowled away by the goddess of pleasure.

To my surprise though, he kept it together pretty well, his cheeks only coloring slightly as she introduced herself. Morpheus seemed to fluster him more, the dream god's unearthly vibe leaving him stammering a bit.

'Please, sit,' Morpheus said, and we all took seats at the grand table. A satyr entered through the open door at the back of the room, carrying a tray of the delicious fizzy wine in saucer glasses.

'Sam, watch out for this stuff, it's not really meant for humans,' I said to him quietly.

'You can heal my hangover,' he grinned at me, and took a big sip. 'Fuck me, that's good!'

'Yeah, all food and drink here is.' I heard the pride in my voice as I spoke, as though I was showing off something that belonged to me. Somewhere along the line, my brain had seemed to have accepted Olympus as my home.

'Persephone, I've asked you here in a somewhat formal capacity,' said Morpheus, and we all looked at him. 'I would like to offer you my services in the chariot race.' I blinked at him. The chariot race. Zeus' words rushed back to me. *I could have two people to help me.*

'Seriously?'

'Yes. Did you have a team in mind already?'

'No, not at all, I hadn't even thought about it yet,' I spluttered. 'You would really risk yourself to help me?'

He chuckled.

'I'm as immortal as you can get without being an Olympian, the risk to me would be minimal,' he said gently. 'And I like Hades. So no offense, but I would be doing it for him, rather than you.'

I beamed at him, my heart swelling in my chest.

'Thank you! Thank you so much!' *I wouldn't be alone.* For the first time in this awful competition, I would have a friend by my side during a Trial. The thought was overwhelming.

'I'm assuming you were going to ask me too,' said Hecate. I snapped my head to her.

'Really?'

'Gods yeah. Same reason as Morpheus. I can't be dealing with a depressed Hades as a boss,' she shrugged. Her voice was as indifferent as her body language, but her eyes sparkled with something else. Excitement? She had been there, with me or near me, every single step of this journey. I'd seen her pale when discovering how dangerous my tasks were, seen the concern in her face when I'd been injured, seen her determination when we trained. She cared about me, I was sure.

'Will I be allowed to have two people from the Underworld to help me? Surely the hell-hounds know you two? I mean, Hades wasn't even allowed to talk to me before the last Trial.'

'Actually, I have the good fortune to never have to deal with the hounds,' said Morpheus dryly.

'I see them every day, but it won't matter. They'll be under Zeus' control, and there's nothing we can tell you about them that will help. And besides, Minthe has an advantage too. She's already done this Trial once.' Hecate said. That sounded more like a punishment than an advantage to me.

'But by that logic, if Eurynomos was under Zeus' control, why wasn't I allowed to talk to you or Hades last night?'

'Many of the demons in the Underworld can be bribed. If you know what to offer them, they'll do anything you ask. The hounds can't be bribed though, they're too well trained.'

'Oh. What does Eurynomos like?'

'Chocolate.'

'You're joking,' I said, staring at Hecate. She shrugged. 'You mean I could have avoided all that shit if I'd just offered him some fucking chocolate?'

'The Underworld is a fucked up place, Persy.'

SIXTEEN

HADES

'Will you put a fucking toga on, this is a formal meeting!' Zeus snapped as I appeared on top of his mountain, at the edge of his sky-high throne room.

'Will you learn to do what you're fucking supposed to, for once?' I barked back. Hera stood up from a long oval table and gave me a pointed stare. I clenched my jaw and changed my clothes to a black toga.

'Thank you, Hades,' Hera said and sat down again, gesturing for me to do the same. It looked like I was the last one to arrive. 'I do not want this meeting to degenerate into an argument,' she said, looking between Zeus and I as I yanked a chair back from the table and sat down, arms folded.

'So, I suppose as usual we are going to pretend that Zeus has done nothing wrong?' I asked. My brother bared his teeth at me but said nothing.

'Zeus acknowledges that Eurynomos was stronger than he first thought.'

'Nobody listens to me,' I spat. 'I've been telling you all for the last hundred years, each Eurynomos gets stronger than the last. It's the same with all the infernal fucking creatures in Virgo!'

'Are you saying you are worried about keeping them under control?' asked Athena.

'No. Absolutely not,' I lied.

'Then what are you saying?'

'That there is a reason they grow in strength. We should be trying to deal with it.'

'We have had this conversation before, it is an Underworld problem, not ours,' said Apollo dismissively.

'I assure you, it is not caused by anything in Virgo. Every sinner who crosses my path fuels the demons, and the number of sinners grows every damned minute. Olympus is filling people with greed and hate, and that is not my doing!' Frustration was coursing through me. How many times did I have to tell them? How could I make them see what they were turning our world into, what the consequences of that would be, without admitting to them how much of my soul I had already lost to the darkness?

'If you become unfit to rule the Underworld, someone must take your place,' said Zeus quietly. Every pair of eyes fell on him.

'Are you volunteering to swap?' I asked him sarcastically. I knew he would never relieve me of this duty. And it was too late anyway. Virgo was a part of me, I was bound to the realm too deeply to ever be severed. If I fell, it would be to the dead. I would become a part of the Underworld itself.

'You would be a poor ruler of the skies, brother,' Zeus said, still not meeting my eyes. 'But I believe I owe you an apology.'

'What?' I wasn't the only one who looked shocked.

'The demons you preside over require more strength than I realized and we failed to heed your warnings. But do not take my admission of your strength as a compliment.'

His eyes finally settled on mine, and they were sparking with electrifying purple energy. Every instinct in my body fired a warning, and power surged through my veins. 'The darkness in that creature was pure destruction. And you must be full of it to have such dominion over him. You are more dangerous than I thought you were.'

I could feel myself growing, the monster awake and ready. If Zeus wanted to know just how dangerous I was, I would show him. Too long he had dismissed me, bullied me. And now he had experienced just a taste of what I dealt with daily, he sought to use it against me?

'You chose one of the strongest demons in my realm for Persephone to face because you wanted to torment me, because you wanted to watch me lose her, and now you are shocked when you discover how strong it is?' I laughed, long and loud, and Zeus's expression darkened further as he grew to match me. 'Brother, you have no idea what I am capable of. What I have always been capable of.' Blue light was rolling from my huge body, forming an army of souls that began lining up around me. 'You made me a king, Zeus. A King of the Dead. And I have all the power that entails.'

'And it will never match mine,' Zeus hissed. 'Just because I can't control your fucking demons does not mean you are stronger than me. You would not be able to control my lightning!'

'Nor could I control Poseidon's waves, but I'm not the one fucking trying to! You behave like a spoiled child who wants to play with everyone else's toys and it will end us all!'

'You started this when you deliberately broke our rules and created the thirteenth realm. This is your doing, not mine.'

'Stop fighting like children!' bellowed Hera suddenly, standing up again. 'Zeus, you have tormented Hades by bringing Persephone back, and now you must deal with that. Hades, your feelings for Persephone are clouding your ability to perform your duties, and *you* must deal with that. Now sit down, both of you.' Her voice rang out so loudly it actually made my head hurt, and the blue army of the dead shimmered and vanished.

Slowly, we both began to shrink back down. I caught the amused look on Dionysus' face and resisted the urge to lash out at him.

'It is extremely important that we do not have a repeat of what happened before. I am referring to when Persephone was sent to Tartarus,' Hera said.

'I agree,' I ground out.

'Then you will understand that you must not watch

the last Trial with us, but guard the entrance to Tartarus instead.'

'What? No! If Zeus loses control of the hell-hounds they could rip her to shreds!'

'Then at least you won't have to watch,' Zeus said with a cruel smile. Before I could leap from my chair at him, Athena stood, thirty feet tall before my ass could leave the seat.

'Enough! Olympus is more important than anything else, and Persephone has the ability to cause the end of it, or plunge us into another endless bloody war. Cronos killed how many immortals before we defeated him last time? And many strong Titan allies who helped before are now gone, and we do not know where. We must not risk his being freed for anything, or anyone.'

'Brother, you can't put one mortal above the safety of the whole of Olympus,' added Poseidon quietly.

My insides churned as I stared between them, my muscles so tense they throbbed. I couldn't argue. What they were saying was true, and if all eleven of them were in agreement...

'What if the one who sent her to Tartarus last time is an Olympian?' I said, playing my last card. Athena visibly flinched and Hera made a scoffing sound. 'It's the only thing that makes sense, who else would know about Cronos? About what happened before?'

Every pair of eyes around the table bore into mine.

'You are so desperate you would accuse us?' asked Apollo, his voice hard. 'Why would any of us want a war after building this place so perfectly?'

Perfect? Was he not listening every time I told them how twisted the souls entering my realm were becoming? Frustration welled through me, teetering on the edge of rage. I had to make them understand. But before I could say anything, Zeus spoke.

'Even if it is one of us, you need to guard Tartarus. You are Cronos' keeper, and you must be there if anything happens.'

'I can flash there in an instant if needed,' I spat.

'An instant might be all Cronos needs. The decision is final.'

SEVENTEEN

PERSEPHONE

The meal Morpheus served us was fantastic. As we ate Sam asked more questions about the Underworld and Hades, but I struggled to concentrate on the conversation. The final Trial was almost here, and then this would be over. The thought of losing, of Hades wed to someone else, caused a surge of something dark and hot to roll through me, unsettling enough that I stopped myself even considering it. I had to win. There was no alternative. I still didn't know how I could live forever in Virgo, but I knew I at least had to be able to try. I ached to talk to Hades, and almost leaped out of my skin when his voice sounded tentatively in my head.

'Persephone?'

'Hades!'

'Am I interrupting?'

'No, never. I miss you,' I told him.

'Good,' he replied, and I swore I could hear a smile in his mental voice.

'Can I come and get you?'
'Please.'

Hades flashed into Morpheus' rooms a second later, and I was surprised to see him in a black toga instead of his jeans. He looked obscenely hot in it, the glimpse of bare chest making me want to reach out and touch him right there. He nodded politely at everyone, and I told him that Hecate and Morpheus were going to ride with me in the chariot. Genuine relief washed over his tense features, and he thanked them both.

'I must prepare Persephone as best I can for tomorrow, so we are leaving now,' he said.

'Code for screwing,' said Skop, and I glared at him. Hades fixed his gaze on the small dog, and his tail stopped wagging.

'Persephone has no need for a guard tonight,' he said. 'You may stay with Hecate.' Hecate made a noise of protest but a look from Hades made her fall silent.

'This could be my last night with Hades,' I told Skop quickly. *'Please.'*

'If anything happens to you, Dionysus will kill me. And not demon-kill me, but actually kill me.'

'What's going to happen to me with the King of the Underworld there to protect me?'

'That's not the point, I'm not supposed to leave your side.'

A long silence filled the room, the mute argument obvious to everyone.

'You can turn back into a gnome and drink this stuff with me if you like. I'm not bothered by your enormous dong,' said Sam, raising a glass at Skop.

'Fine,' Skop said after a second's hesitation. *'That sounds fair.'*

I shook my head with a smile. All it took was some booze to buy his cooperation.

'I'll see you all tomorrow then,' I said, and kissed my brother on the cheek.

'I need the low-down on these mutts of yours,' I said to Hades, once he had flashed us to his rooms. 'And then I need the low-down on this extremely sexy toga of yours...' I made my voice as seductive as I could, but frowned when I saw his expression. 'What's wrong?'

'So many things,' he said, and his words were laden with strain.

'Tell me.'

'I can't-' he began, shaking his head, but I cut him off with an ineffectual shove to his chest. I ignored the electrifying feel of his skin on my hands and put on my fiercest face.

'I am not taking anymore of this *'I can't'* bullshit. I don't know if you noticed, but I killed a demon today. I have stopped asking you about my past, as you requested, and am doing everything I can to embrace my future. With you. As Queen of the god-damned Underworld. Do not fucking tell me that I do not need to know or you can't tell me, or I swear I'll lose that damned Trial tomorrow on purpose.'

I was expecting anger or rebuttal from him, but relief washed over his face, the tense anger softening and making him irresistibly beautiful. Before I could stop myself I stood up on tiptoes and kissed him. He kissed me back, softly, and too briefly.

'You are right, and we should talk. Now. If we keep kissing, then there will be very little talking.' Desire flashed through his eyes and I stepped backwards, nodding. He was right. If his lips were on mine a second longer I would be tearing off his toga with my teeth.

We sat down together in his living room, and he took a long breath. I didn't know if I was supposed to, but I felt nervous. I mean, what could he tell me that was worse than Cronos wanting to use me to destroy Olympus? Was he going to tell me what I did before, to get sent away? A weird mix of desperation to know and fear that once I found out I wouldn't want to, skittered through me and I wrung my hands together.

'If you win the Trial tomorrow, you will become my Queen. And when you ruled beside me before, I shared everything with you. It would be folly not to share what I know with you now.'

'I'm glad you're seeing sense,' I said tersely. He gave me a look that said 'don't push it,' and continued.

'You have seen the darkness in me,' he said. It wasn't a question. 'That darkness comes from the souls who pass through here who have sinned. I began to lose my faith in life, and the darkness took root. Each year, the number of terrible things I pass judgment on increases. The number of sinners increases. The crimes worsen. The greed and hatred of mortals appears boundless and infinite.' The look on his face caused a lump to swell in my throat. The strain he carried... *Infinite.* His endless future was to be exposed to the very worst of people. 'I am worried, Persephone, and I can not tell my Olympian brethren the true consequences of my concerns. The world they rule celebrates greed, exemplifies selfishness, encourages hatred. Eventually the darkness will win and the Underworld will claim me.'

My heart was hammering in my chest as I listened to him. What was he telling me?

'If Zeus knew how strong the beast inside me was, he would find a new ruler of the Underworld, rather than risking me lose control. And he is beginning to suspect. But even if he does that, I will not be able to leave. Too much of myself is in the very rock around us, and too much of the essence of Virgo lives within me. My bond to this place is final and unbreakable.'

'What would you become then?'

'The thing you saw when you came back from New York. Forever. And I would be far too powerful to be free. Zeus would have to imprison me in Tartarus.'

'No,' I said, aghast. 'No, you couldn't live there!'

'It wouldn't be me anymore.'

'We can't let this happen. We'll make them understand, make them change how they rule Olympus!'

'Persephone, I have been asking them for centuries. It is too late. You can't just make the world nicer.'

'Then my magic will save you!' Tears were spilling down my cheeks now, memories of the mindless violence I had felt from him when the monster had taken over twisting through me.

'Yes. Your ability to nurture life, to share your light... It heals me. Only you can keep my soul safe.'

'Hades, even if I lose and you have to marry that witch, I will do anything to keep you safe,' I whispered.

'But Zeus was right about you living here. Eventually the darkness will put out your light. You are made to thrive in nature, not under the ground, encased in rock.' Pain filled his voice.

I stared at him.

'So... If I stay here and keep you alive, I die?'

'You will lose your soul to this place, just like everyone else here. And with it, lose the power to heal me.'

A small sob bubbled out of my throat before I could stop it, and he wrapped his huge arms around me. I knew with every fiber in my being that I would rather die than watch him be lost to Tartarus.

'We'll find a way to stop it. We'll find a way to stop so much bad happening in the world.' I knew I sounded naive, but I didn't care. I had nothing else. Hades stroked a hand down my hair, his sturdy warmth an anchor for my churning thoughts.

'My Queen, we have many obstacles to face before we even get to that. As long as you live in the Under-

world, in proximity to Cronos, the other Gods will inter-
fere. They want me to guard Tartarus tomorrow, instead
of watching the Trial with them.'

'What? Why?' I pulled out of his embrace to look
at him.

'They are worried about another sabotage.'

'But you think it's one of them?'

'Perhaps, yes. And so does Poseidon.'

'Which one?'

'I don't know. Honestly, I can't see a reason any of
them would want to start a war or destroy Virgo.'

Hades fell silent and I blew out a sigh, trying to reign
in my emotions.

'What if Zeus loses control again?' I asked him.

'I have thought about this hard,' he said, and there
was steel in his voice. 'It will make more sense if I tell
you about my dogs first.' I raised my eyebrows, an invitation to continue. 'Cerberus is the most well-known. I
found him as a pup in the depths of the Underworld,
born to monsters now trapped in Tartarus. In those
lonely early days he was my only friend.' I felt a pang
of love for Hades so strong I almost interrupted him to
kiss him, but instead I sat on my hands and listened
carefully. 'Cerberus ended up being the first of three
dogs, and though the other two are not as dangerous as
him, they are both lethal in their own way. They are
called Fonax and Olethros. When you lived here, you
spent two years bonding with them, and though it was a
test of patience, they came to trust you eventually.
Cerberus took the longest to come round, but actually,

he ended up the most fond of you.' A lop-sided smile pulled at the corner of Hades' mouth. 'Back then you had enough power to survive your early attempts at making friends with them. I'm praying you do again now.'

'Surely I've got a better chance than Minthe,' I said, optimistically. 'They might remember me.'

'The river Lethe is a powerful thing. I doubt that it was any less effective at wiping the dog's memories than everyone else's.'

'Speaking of which,' I said, casually. 'Where is the river Lethe?'

'Persephone, you must never go there. I swear to you, it will only bring you pain.'

Frustration simmered and settled in my gut.

'Do you intend to keep this secret from me our entire lives?' *What would be left of them when the godforsaken Underworld had stripped our souls bare.*

'Yes. As *you* asked me to.' I rolled my eyes. He was never going to tell me. For the briefest moment I considered again telling him about the Atlas garden and the stranger, but I knew he would disapprove, and I wasn't willing to close off the only access to information about my past I had. It wasn't that I didn't trust Hades, but I hadn't made up my mind yet. The need to know what the old me was capable of was impossible to snuff out completely. Plus the stranger said even Hades didn't know the full story. If there was a chance I wasn't guilty of whatever the gods thought I was, then at some point I had to try to find out the truth.

Just not before I survived the hell-hounds and won the Hades Trials.

'Cerberus normally does my bidding exactly,' said Hades. 'But if my asshole brother loses control of him, he'll be operating on instinct alone, and that is to guard my realm. I do not believe that he will attack if you are not near the gates of Virgo. The other two will be guarding something else, I don't know what, but the same principle should apply.'

'OK. So get away from the gates or whatever the dog is guarding if it all goes to shit?'

'Yes.'

'I can do that.'

'And win.'

'I *have* to do that. You said I could have a cat if I win.' Hades cocked his head at me, the tension easing from his face.

'As long as it's a scary, Underworld-appropriate cat.'

'Woah now, there were no caveats before! I want something cute and fluffy.' He scowled at me.

'No cat is cute.'

'That is simply not true.'

'Hmmm. I remain unconvinced. You'll have to win in order to prove it to me.'

I grinned at him, forcing the nerves and pressure down. If he couldn't watch the Trial, I wanted him to be as confident in me as possible.

'No problem. I'm a badass goddess now, in case you hadn't noticed.'

'Persephone,' he said, touching my cheek. His silver

eyes changed, the teasing gleam replaced with that heart-breaking intensity I had seen when I first laid eyes on him. 'I won't watch your light go out. Ever.'

'And I won't watch the darkness take you. Together we will be strong enough.'

His lips moved to mine, gentle and hot. He scooped me up, standing. He carried me to the bedroom, then sat down on the bed, his lips never ceasing their caress, his tongue teasing me. Heat was pooling inside me as the intensity of the kiss grew and my head filled with what I knew was coming.

My feet found the floor and I pulled away from him, standing up breathlessly. I tugged him to his feet and reached up to his shoulder, slowly pulling at his toga. It didn't move, and he smiled a delicious, predatory smile.

'You know, these aren't easy to take off.'

'Well, I need you to. Take it off. I need you to take it off,' I said thickly. 'If there's the slightest chance this is the last time I see you, then you need to be naked for as much of it as possible.'

With a small shimmer, his toga was gone. I sucked in a breath, biting down on my lip as my eyes flicked straight to his arousal. *Good gods.*

'Your turn,' he breathed, and I felt a whisper of air across my body as my own clothes vanished.

I stepped into him, and he wrapped his arms tightly around me as we fell backwards onto the bed, lips locked in a kiss more hungry than the last.

'I will never get enough of you,' I told him, as he rolled me over, so he was on top of me.

'I want you to see what I see,' he said, his eyes dark and his voice thick with desire. I tugged my hand out of his hair, and a gold vine crept from my palm. Slowly, it reached his muscular arm, coiling around his hard bicep. Gold vine tattoos began to spread across his skin, and heat and desire and love rushed into me.

For a moment I saw myself as he did, glowing with glittering light, skin like honey and face perfect. A beacon in the dark. Then I felt him push against me, and every muscle in my body clenched with desire. Passion, his and mine, exploded inside me, concentrated between my legs.

'I love you,' he said, and then he was inside me, and the pleasure that rocked through him wasn't just mirrored in my own body, it flowed into me through the gold vine.

Being with me was more than physical to him, it was as deep, and as real and true as it was for me. Knowing how much he wanted me, loved me, *needed me,* was the most intense aphrodisiac I'd ever experienced. Our bodies moved together, utterly in sync, slowing when we got exquisitely close, speeding up when passion overwhelmed us. I lost myself not just in the pleasure, but in the shared feeling, the knowledge that we were made for one another.

The pleasure, the power, the bliss grew until it filled us, each touch of his lips on my skin, the feel of his hot breath on my neck, his fingers on my ribs and breasts as intense as his thrusts, until it was too much to contain.

We let go at the same time, and there was nothing but him and sensation, my body part of his.

He held me as I shuddered against him, my nails digging into his back as he pressed his face against mine.

'You are mine, and I am yours,' I breathed into his hair.

'Always, my Queen.'

EIGHTEEN

PERSEPHONE

'Why can't you just show me a map?' I asked Hecate as she tried to explain to me what the Judgment Hall was and what it looked like. She'd been trying to teach me the key monuments of the Underworld for what felt like hours, and I was still having trouble laying it out in my head.

'Argh, Persephone, pay attention! Everything in the Underworld moves around all the time, the rivers are alive. The only constants are the things I'm trying to tell you!'

'Morpheus is driving and you'll be with me, why do I need to know?' Under any other circumstance I would love to have learned about Virgo, but with less than an hour before the Trial began, nothing was getting through my nerves and into my skull. I was practically vibrating with energy. Possibly against my better judgment, I had eaten the last seed. Unlike all of the other times I could feel the difference, swirling energy pulsing through my veins, desperate to latch onto something. I almost felt like I needed to grow my own body, become bigger, in lieu of being able to make anything else burst to life.

'You need to know in case anything happens, or you get lost,' ground out Hecate.

'I'm sorry, I just can't concentrate. I need to do something. Do you want to train?'

'No, you need to save your power.'

'Hello?' called Morpheus from the other side of Hecate's closed door. My brother groaned from where he lay on the other sofa, a pillow over his head.

'Serves you right,' I told him as Hecate leaped up to open the door.

'Heal my hangover, please,' he moaned. I rolled my eyes, and sent my vine out towards him. He jumped in surprise when it coiled around his limp wrist, then yelped as I sent my magic toward him.

'That feels weird as fuck!'

'Yeah, well, it works so quit moaning.' The vine disintegrated as Morpheus strode into the room. His swirling skin was positively glowing.

'Are you ready?' he asked me enthusiastically. 'Because the chariot is, and I want you to see it before we start.' A bolt of excitement shot through me and I jumped to my feet.

'Definitely.'

'Can I come?' said Sam, struggling to a sitting position, the pillow sliding off him.

'No,' I said. 'Shit, who's going to stay with him whilst

you're with me?' I asked, whirling to Hecate, panicking suddenly.

'Calm down, Hedone has volunteered.' With a sigh of relief I looked to Sam.

'Just in case I do die, give me a hug,' I told him. He pulled a face as he stood up, wrapping his arms around me.

'I saw what you did to that gross thing in the cave, you're going to do great,' he said. 'And once this is done, we can talk about what happens next, yeah?' he added quietly, looking down at me.

'Yes. I promise.'

'Good. 'Cos cool as it is here, I need some sunshine.'

'You and me both,' I said, squeezing him.

'Good luck, Persy.' He kissed me on the top of my head and let me go. A fresh wave of trepidation rolled over me as I moved to Hecate, and she flashed me, Skop and Morpheus out of her rooms.

I found myself in a bare, rocky cavern, the walls glowing with artificial daylight. Set in the middle of the narrow space was a wooden chariot and I felt my eyes widen as I took it in. It looked sort of like the pictures of ancient Greek ones I'd seen in my classes, except the front was raised and peaked exactly like the front of a small boat, and there were no wheels. In fact, it looked a bit like someone had cut a boat in half and made the bottom flat. The decoration and the grand spiral trim across the wood looked every bit ancient Greek. There was no back to it at all, the wooden planks making up the base just stopping dead. Six foot-long spikes jutted out of each side of it, and attached at intervals on the high sides were chains with angry looking spiked balls. My memory flashed on the skeleton and the flail I'd used in my very first Trial. It seemed appropriate to have a flail in my last Trial too.

'It's awesome, Morpheus,' grinned Hecate, walking around it slowly. 'Persy, whatever you do, don't fall off the back.'

I blinked at her, then nodded mutely. It looked like it would be a pretty tight squeeze for three people.

'Shall we take her to the start line?' Morpheus looked at me. His eyes were alive with excitement. The tiniest bit of me resented him for it. For me, this was not a game. It was life or death, and more than he knew besides.

But more of me was grateful for his help. I mean, where the hell would I have found a chariot? Least of all had the time to learn to control one.

'Definitely,' I told him.

'Step aboard.' He gestured at the wooden vehicle.

This was it. I patted my dagger at my side, and stroked my hand over the pocket I had put Poseidon's pearl in, checking it was still there. I'd worn the leather corset today, deciding protection was more important than maneuverability. My hair was braided out of my face and my boots were laced tightly. I had nothing left to do. I was ready.

With a big breath, I gripped the side of the chariot and stepped onto the planks. Morpheus strode up beside me, positioning himself at the front, where the wooden sides met in a sharp peak. The prow, I supposed.

Hecate hopped on behind me.

'Hold on,' she grinned, and the chariot lifted off the rocky ground.

I suppressed the yelp that tried to escape my throat, and gripped the side hard. Just like the ships soaring around Mount Olympus, the boat shaped chariot was flying, on mind-power alone. We hovered for a moment, and Morpheus looked back at me, his skin sparkling.

'Ready?'

'Uhuh,' I replied, pulse racing and heart hammering. With a whoop from Hecate, the chariot raced forward.

For a terrifying moment I thought we were going to smash straight into the cavern wall, but as we approached it, an opening started to form in the rock. We burst through and shock stilled my nerves as the most incredible view materialized before me. With a jolt, I registered what I was looking at.

The Underworld.

All the time I had been living in Virgo I'd been flashed between rooms, and although I'd seen many places; my bedroom, the throne room, the training room, the conservatory, the ballroom, the breakfast room, even Tartarus, I'd never been able to imagine Virgo as an actual realm. It had just been a series of caverns and pits to me, and the way it was all connected had just been a vague description from Hecate.

But the view I had as we soared through the air in the chariot...

It was as though we were in a giant cavern, one as large as a city, and as mountainous as the Rockies. We were flying over a river of blue light, similar to the light that came from Hades when he was in god mode. The river was gouged from the dark rock and it seemed to have sources everywhere, waterfalls of light pouring down the many slopes into the main, rushing body of water. On my left and dominating the landscape was a towering mountain, and at its peak, a palace. *Hades' palace.* I felt my jaw drop further. Huge skulls, visible for miles, were carved into the walls and fierce gothic-style towers and balustrades were wrapped with thorned rose carvings. The very tip of the palace reached up past the ceiling of the cavern, and I realized with a start that that must be where the rooms with windows were, the rooms that were above ground. The breakfast room.

As I dragged my eyes down from the palace I saw a glowing band wrapped around the middle of the mountain, shimmering gold. As I squinted into the light I realized there was an island floating just off the mountain.

'That's Elysium, and the Isle of the Blessed. Where the good guys go,' said Hecate, reaching past me and pointing.

'I can't see clearly,' I said, and she laughed.

'The only way you can see into paradise is by dying,

so be careful what you wish for. Over there you can just see the river of fire, Phlegethon, that leads down to Tartarus.' She pointed at the flicker of red far in the distance. 'And down there are the Fields of Asphodel and the Judgment Hall. Where the dead come to be judged.' She pointed below us. I peered hesitantly down, over the side of the chariot. My head swam for a moment, but I dragged my healing power up and around me, forcing out my body's reaction to the height. I simply couldn't let vertigo affect me in this Trial. It wasn't an option. I was a damned goddess, and I was in charge of my own body. My vision steadied as I channeled my power, and I took long breaths as I focused.

Below me was a massive washed-out meadow. Hundreds upon hundreds of figures ambled slowly around, and though we were too high to make out details, I could see no color. A gleaming white temple sat between the blue river and another one that glowed purple until it merged with the blue.

'What are these rivers?' I asked.

'The big blue one is the Styx. She's hatred and honesty. The purple one is Acheron, who is woe.'

'Nice,' I mumbled.

'The river Cocytus is over there today. That's lamen-tation.' She pointed at a green glowing river streaming through an uneven section of rock far to our right.

'And the Lethe?' Hecate shrugged.

'She's always a bitch to find.'

'What color is she?'

'Can't remember,' Hecate grinned at me. 'And I've given up trying to. That's her power, after all.'

'It's quite beautiful,' I said, staring out at it all. 'If a little dark.'

'Yeah. I think so too. See over there? That's the main entrance, for folk who can't flash. That's where Cerberus guards the gates and the ferryman collects the dead.' She was pointing to the top of the cavern, at the opposite end of the river Styx to the palace, where the river seemed to disappear into the rock.

'OK. So where will we be racing?'

'The starting point is the Judgment Hall,' said Morpheus without turning around. We were dropping in height, the spectacular view disappearing as high outcrops of dark rock grew up around us as we moved lower.

'Where are the demon's lairs, like the Empusa and Eurynomos?' I asked Hecate.

'They move around, but they're all hidden throughout the rock.' I stared down at the dark, jagged surface as we raced over it. There could be any kind of creature right below us, and I wouldn't know.

'How do you find them?'

'I'm tethered to them, like Hades. They are bound to us.'

'Would... Would they be bound to me if I became Queen here?'

'No. You'd be giving yourself to Hades, not Virgo.'

I thought about what Hades had told me the night before. He said he was part of Virgo, that he and the

Underworld were one now. So maybe Hecate was wrong, and if I gave myself to Hades in marriage, I would be wedding the Underworld too. If I became his Queen, perhaps I *would* have dominion in this place.

Did I want that? Did I want to know what was hidden in the rock, in this dark and toxic place? If it was a part of Hades, then I must embrace it. But it felt so very far from any part of me.

I was saved from my thoughts when the gleaming white temple loomed before us. It was massive, at least three stories tall, and just like all the throne rooms it had no walls. The left and right sides had a tight row of columns holding up the triangular roof, and the other two sides were completely open, allowing Morpheus to glide the chariot into the building. We landed gently on the white marble floor and my gaze fixed on the chariot we had pulled up next to.

NINETEEN

PERSEPHONE

I t looked exactly how I would expect a chariot belonging to Minthe to look. Where the wood of mine was a rich and natural hue, hers was painted a dark, angry red. Instead of square Greek spirals, hers was decorated with a fierce looking eagle, the wings of the bird stretching intimidatingly around each side of the chariot. There were big pointed spikes jutting out of each side like mine, but where I had flails she had ropes with red sacks tied to the end. I frowned at them, then scanned the rest of the temple as I stepped off the wood and onto the marble. I could see row upon row of stepped benches, set up like bleachers along the right side of the space, and the dais with the twelve thrones was on the other side. In front of the dais was the grand table that the three judges were always sitting at when they appeared. I couldn't see any other people.

'Where is everyone?' I asked as Morpheus followed me out of the chariot.

'I'm not sure. I'll go look,' he said, and strode towards the dais. Hecate followed him.

'They're waiting for you,' Minthe's voice rang out, and she stepped out from behind one of the pillars. She was wearing an outfit similar to mine, but the leather was a rich burgundy color and her hair was loose around her shoulders. 'They can't start without their precious human underdog,' she said, her voice dripping with menace.

'Seriously, you're still going to be this shitty to me? After I saved your damned life?'

'I've wanted immortality longer than I've been indebted to you,' she spat. 'If your pathetic conscious didn't allow you to kill me in order to win outright, then I deserve every chance I've got at winning the prize.'

'The *prize* is a man,' I said angrily. 'With a heart and soul and feelings and-'

She cut me off with a hiss.

'Save it, Persephone. You may not be capable of killing me, but I don't believe you're so sweet and inno-cent that you think the King of the Dead is capable of love.' Fury swept hot through me and I felt my lips curl back from my teeth.

'You don't deserve him,' I hissed.

'Not true. Whoever wins the Trials deserves the prize.'

'Stop calling him a fucking prize!' I shouted, and my vines burst from my palms toward her. Chunks of dark rock flew between the columns, knocking my vines away before they reached her and I whipped them back with a snarl.

'My powers belong down here,' she said, and the rocks flew back past her, out of the temple. 'Yours do not.'

I felt my vines falter at her words. They were true. I was out of my depth. I didn't belong here.

She could make the very rock of the Underworld fly about with her mountain magic, and all I had was freaking plants. *Plants that heal the soul of the man you love. The man who loves you.* I clung to the inner voice, and my vines flicked taut again.

'I won't be bullied, Minthe. Not by you or Zeus, or anyone else.'

'I'm not a bully. I'm a competitor, just like you.'

She was right, this *was* a competition. And she was goading me, I realized. Trying to damage my confidence, trying to throw me off before we started.

Two could play at that game. I pulled my vines back, straightening my shoulders.

'Good luck, then,' I said, as sincerely as I could manage. She frowned at me. 'You're not going to win, but I hope you survive, so that dealing with that demon wasn't a complete waste of time.' Minthe cocked her head at me.

'I owe you nothing, Persephone,' she said quietly. But I could hear in her voice that she knew the words weren't true.

'May the best woman win, Minthe,' I said, and strode after my friends.

~

Morpheus and Hecate couldn't find anyone to ask what we were supposed to do next, so I sent a tentative thought to Hades.

'Where are you?' I asked him.

'We will arrive in ten minutes,' he answered immediately. *'My egotistical brother wants the gods to make an entrance.'* The strain was clear in his mental voice.

'OK. See you soon.' I bit my bottom lip, and added quickly, *'I love you.'* There was a slight pause, and then he answered, the tension in his tone gone completely.

'I love you too, my Queen.'

Biting back my grin, I told the others we had to wait and we made our way back to the chariot. Only a few moments later, spectators began appearing in the bleachers. Within five minutes, the space was full. Creatures and humans of every size, shape and color crammed in together, and the chatter was at fever pitch.

'Fucking tourists,' grumbled Hecate. 'There's a reason Hades keeps this place secret.' I raised my eyebrows at her and she leaned back on the side of the chariot. 'If you glamorize the Underworld, who the fuck is going to be scared of ending up here? Damned idiots.'

I could tell Hecate was more nervous than she was letting on, not least because of the amount of times she was saying the work fuck in a sentence. I was pretty sure we shared the habit of swearing profusely when nervous or angry.

'Is that a cyclops?' I asked, pointing at a giant woman in the bleachers with one large amber eye and sharp spikes sticking out through her hair, covering her head.

'Yeah. Don't see 'em often, they're usually in Hephaestus' forges, and his realm is forbidden.' She scowled. 'As this realm is supposed to be.'

There was a bright flash of white light, and we both turned to the dais. Eleven of the twelve gods were there, all looking exceptionally grand. There were all in togas, even Dionysus, and they all wore large crowns. Hera's was the most eye catching, adorned with peacock feathers, and Athena's was the most plain, just a gold band.

'Good day, Olympus!' boomed the commentator, his voice seemingly amplified by the rock around us. I spotted him next to the judges' table, and started as I realized the three judges were now there, eyes intent on Minthe and I. 'Please welcome your host for these incredible Trials one last time!'

Black smoke suddenly billowed through the area, and the crowd gasped as it began to gather in front of the dais, a small tornado forming. It began to solidify as blue light flickered through the air, lighting up the smoke like a strobe light. An enormous two-pronged trident made of gleaming onyx emerged from the swirling smoke, then the smoky form of a man followed it, at least ten feet tall.

'This is the grand entrance you were talking about?' I said mentally to Hades as the crowd erupted into cheers.

'It was not my fucking idea,' he ground out.

'You look impressive,' I told him. The smoke figure raised the trident and blue light shot from the end like fireworks. The cheers got louder.

'Impressive? I'm supposed to be terrifying, not impressive. I could make every unwelcome person in this hall *feel their worst fears right now,'* he hissed. *'Instead, Zeus turns me into a jester with tricks and lights.'* His words were laced with bitterness, and I understood his anger. Zeus was turning the King of the Dead, Lord of the Underworld, into a spectacle, whilst showing the world the realm he had always striven to keep private.

'Maybe give them a little taste of what you can do,' I said, and saw his smoke form pause.

'Really?'

'Just a little. Don't make anyone actually mess themselves.' I heard a tiny chuckle, then cold rippled over me and the cheers died out abruptly. Tendrils of something pricked at my skin, and discomfort and fear started to seep into my mind, but my healing magic leaped up around me. Within a second, the fear had been forced out, barred from me completely.

When the room was silent, Zeus stood. His expression was tight.

'Thank you, brother, for that welcome,' he said tersely. Hades flickered, and reappeared on his throne. His smoke form looked languid and relaxed. I didn't know if he got pleasure from frightening people or what that said about him, but I *did* know he got pleasure from defying Zeus. And that was worth freaking out a few morbid spectators.

'Thank you, Zeus,' Hades said, his voice slithery and creepy. It was so weird now to hear him speak like that, his rich, warm tones nowhere to be heard. 'The race is along the Styx, to the gates of Virgo. You will encounter all three hell-hounds on the way, ending with Cerberus.

Each dog is guarding a gem. Green for Persephone, red for Minthe. Collect all the gems first and you will win.'

A massive swell of nerves rolled through me. His cold, impassive voice was so completely at odds with how I knew he felt, but he sounded for all the world like he didn't give a shit which of us won. Doubt stabbed at my mind, until I heard his voice, his real voice, in my mind.

'Win for me, my Queen.'

'I will.'

'I have to leave now. A smoke dummy will be in my place so that the crowd don't know.'

Hecate and Morpheus were climbing onto the chariot and two people had joined Minthe. I couldn't look anywhere other than him though. I didn't want him to leave.

'OK,' I said, stumbling as I stepped onto my chariot. My eyes were locked on his smoke form, adrenaline now rushing through my body. *'I love you.'*

'I love you,' he replied. I felt him leave, the bond pulsing with a faint sense of loss inside me as he moved further from me.

'Shit,' muttered Hecate beside me, and I dragged my eyes from the fake smoke figure now on Hades' throne.

'What's wrong?' I asked her.

'That,' she said, pointing to Minthe's chariot. 'That's what's wrong. Fucking look at them!'

I took a deep breath, anxiety making me feel sick as I took in Minthe's team mates.

The woman at the front of the chariot was wearing a toga and looked about a hundred years old, but that wasn't what I noticed first. She was see-through. Like actually transparent. And the other woman on the chariot was at least six feet tall, wearing a wonder-woman type outfit made of gleaming armor, and holding a cross-bow. Her blonde hair was in a knot on top of her head and the muscles cording her arms and shoulders put my brother's to shame.

'What are they?'

'The woman at the front is an Eidolon. That's a ghost in your world.'

'I thought you controlled ghosts?'

'The ones down here, I do. Not the ones that are free. Like her.'

'And the woman who looks like a body-builder?'

'Definitely an Amazon warrior. But they never leave their tribe in Ares' realm so she must be an outcast.' I raised my eyebrows at the fierce looking woman as she examined her weapon.

'Amazon warriors? Is there anything Olympus doesn't have?'

'Not really. Most history from your world is based on Olympus. What Athena planted as Greek mythology.'

The woman noticed me staring at her before I could answer, and bared her teeth at me.

'Are you ready to face the sting of my bolts?' she called, lifting the crossbow threateningly toward me. My old instinct would have been to flinch away or look to Hecate to help, but my power crackled and hummed in response to the threat and before I could stop myself I lifted my hands.

'Just try it,' I shouted, and black vines whipped from my palms, stopping just short of her and flicking back. The woman's eyes narrowed, but she kept her mouth shut and lowered the weapon.

'Save it for the race, Sanape,' said Minthe, tugging her elbow. Sanape glared at me, then turned away.

'I'm glad to see so much of the old Persephone survived the mortal world,' said Hecate quietly. 'You can't get by in Olympus without a decent dose of courage.'

'You call it courage, the rest of us call it attitude,' said Morpheus with a grin. 'Are you both ready?'

I nodded, and the chariot rose slowly into the air, my stomach lurching with it.

This was it. The final time I would have to fight for my life and the right to marry the man I loved. The man it turned out I had always loved. The man I had been waiting for my whole life, without even knowing it.

Hades' face filled my mind, and strength coursed through me, my power crackling under my skin.

I was going to win this, and become his Queen.

TWENTY

HADES

Not being able to watch Persephone was torture. But even if something terrible did happen, I wouldn't be able to help her, I was bound by the rules of the Trials.

I snarled as I looked out over the rocky landscape to where I knew she was. Perhaps if the chariots got high enough I would be able to see them from here. I knew I was too far away, but I clung to the thought all the same.

Something *was* going to happen, I was sure. There was no way that whoever was trying to punish her or get to Cronos was going to let their last chance go without trying again. At the thought of Cronos I looked along the flaming river, flowing into the mouth of the cave that led to Tartarus. Where Persephone had come back, and stopped me walking into Tartarus while the darkness had control of me. Where she had saved me.

Movement caught my eye and I froze, only relaxing when I realized it was the flickering flames of the river

Phlegethon against the rock walls. I was still holding the onyx trident, a relic I rarely used any more. It had been made for me by Hephaestus, to celebrate the three brothers taking their roles in sky, sea and earth. A trident for each of us. Poseidon hardly went anywhere without his, but I no longer needed the amplification of power it could give me. If anything, I needed less power, not more.

Except today. If anyone was coming for Persephone, they would have to get past me, and I'd take all the strength I could get. I tipped the trident towards the cave mouth.

'You hear that, Cronos? You're not getting your hands on her today, or any other day,' I said, then blew out a frustrated sigh. Being stuck here was 'bullshit', as Persephone had called it.

'Where's the fun in that?' purred a voice.

I had the trident in both hands, pointed directly at the cave mouth in a flash, my form growing fast as a small figure sauntered out of the cave. Nothing should ever be coming out of Tartarus without my permission. The monster reared up inside me, fear and strength swelling me as my heart began to pound.

Ankhiale stepped fully out of the cave, and gave me a low bow. Her red hair burst into flame as she straightened and smiled at me. My blood ran cold as I stared at her.

'How? How have you escaped?' If she was free, did that mean... 'Where is Cronos?'

'King Cronos is safe and sound,' she said. 'My friend couldn't break through his bonds. But he didn't have too much trouble with mine.'

Blue light burst to life around me, and the monster crawled higher up my chest. Ankhiale was ancient. She was one of the strongest Titans in Tartarus. Nobody but me should be able to free her from Tartarus.

'Who?' I demanded. 'Who freed you?' Even as I barked the words though, I knew. Fear squeezed my chest, the darkness twisting and snarling to be free.

'That's not important, little Hades,' she said, and cackled as she grew, eclipsing my size in an instant. Heat so intense it made me wince slammed into me. My eyes flicked to the rows and rows of blue soldiers surrounding me, more getting to their feet from the pool of blue light flowing to the ground from my body. 'What is important is that in a few hours, Cronos, the true King of the Gods, will be free and this shit-hole you call home will be obliterated.'

'Never,' I growled. 'He will never be free while I live.'

'I'm afraid that's not true,' she said, cocking her head and giving me a mocking smile. 'It's your lovely wife who needs to die, not you. You will live on without her, a mindless monster doing your master's bidding.'

'No!' I roared, rage blinding me, horror at the thought of Persephone's death too much to bear. I couldn't lose her. I would do whatever it took. Ankhiale threw her head back and laughed, as flames burst to life across her skin.

'Yes, little Lord,' she said, and launched herself at me.

TWENTY-ONE

PERSEPHONE

'Just some clarifications of the rules, folks, and we can get this race started!' sang the commentator. 'There will be no mental communication allowed during the race. Minthe, follow the red lights, Persephone, follow the green lights. Stay on your own course. This will ensure you don't face the first two dogs at the same time. Only Persephone and Minthe may get the gem from the dog. If anyone else helps, the team will be disqualified and severely punished. After Fonax and Olethros it's a straight race to Cerberus and the finish line!'

I blinked as a dancing green light shimmered into life in front of our chariot, hovered a moment, then bounced out of the temple. An identical red light did the same thing before Minthe.

'Follow the light,' repeated Morpheus. 'No problem.'

'On the gong, you may start,' said the commentator, and the crowd cheered.

'Come on, Persy!' My brother's voice carried over them all, and I looked down to see him and Hedone waving from the front row of the bleachers.

As the gong sounded and the commentator bellowed, 'Go!', rage flared inside me, Hades' primal power surging through the bond.

'Hecate,' I gasped as the chariot shot forward, and I gripped the wooden sides. She didn't hear me over the roar of the crowd, or the rushing of air as we pelted out of the temple, soaring over the glittering blue river. Another swell of fear and fury rolled through my body, mingling with my own adrenaline-fueled energy.

'Duck,' Hecate yelled, and a crossbow bolt thudded into the wood just an inch from my white knuckles.

'Something is happening to Hades,' I shouted, and the chariot swerved slightly as Morpheus looked back at me, his face anxious.

'He can handle himself, Persy, now get down!' she shouted back. Her eyes turned milky as blue light shot from her palms, and my mouth fell open in dumb confusion as I watched the light hit the red chariot ten feet from us. Sanape stumbled, but kept her firm grip on the crossbow.

'Hold on!' shouted Morpheus, and the chariot swerved hard to the left as the red and green lights ahead of us parted abruptly. Minthe's chariot soared off to the right, and I spun to Hecate.

'Something bad is happening, I can feel it!'

'There's nothing you can do from here, Persy!' she said, gripping my arm and looking into my eyes. 'He's one of the strongest beings in Olympus, the best thing you can do for him is concentrate on surviving and winning this.'

I nodded. She was right. Hades could handle anything, and little would be worse for him *or* me than losing the Trials and not being with him.

A geyser of blue liquid shot up past the chariot and Morpheus jerked it aside violently enough for me to almost lose my hold of the wooden side. Heart in my mouth, I tightened my grip and widened my stance.

Dying. Dying would be worse than losing.

'OK. Full focus, I got it,' I told Hecate, breathing deeply in a bid to try to settle my stomach.

My braid whipped over my shoulder as I turned to the front and concentrated on what was before us. We were following the dancing green light along a narrow offshoot of the Styx, and I turned briefly to see the red light in the distance, Minthe's chariot whizzing along after it over a different blue stream of the Styx. The rock around us was uneven to the point of mountainous, and as I looked ahead again, I realized the light was moving lower, forcing us closer to the river. Uneasiness washed over me. Now that my fear of heights was under control, it was actually better to be higher up, as we could see further across the Underworld. The lower we got, the more the rocky slopes obscured our view. Something dark loomed before us and the light swerved towards it, along the glowing river below.

It was a large ridge, and the river was flowing into a cave mouth set low into it.

'Wanna bet either Fonax or Olethros is in there?' called Hecate.

'Bring it on,' I called back, the false bravado not helping my nerves at all.

I couldn't help holding my breath as we entered the darkness of the cave. I was instantly reminded of when I'd been in Tartarus, everything lit by the glow of the flickering river, only this time it was blue instead of red. The bouncing green light ahead of us whizzed along the banks of the Styx, and Morpheus led us after it.

'Any last minute tips on dealing with hell-hounds?' I asked Hecate, my pulse racing.

'Don't get eaten?'

'Thanks.'

My heart skipped a beat as the chariot dipped suddenly, and a new color seeped through the darkness. Purple. Hecate had said the purple river was Acheron, which was woe. 'What happens if we fall in a river?' I asked as mildly as I could.

'The Styx would strip your skin bare in an instant. It's filled with the hatred of every dead soul in Olympus and is toxic as fuck.'

'And the Acheron?'

'You'd become so overwhelmed with sadness you would instantly go mad.'

'Right. Good to know.'

'Just don't fall in the Phlegethon. You don't want to know what happens if you do that.'

I shuddered just thinking about the flaming river.

'Guys,' called Morpheus over his shoulder. The green light was slowing down, drifting toward an island of solid rock between the two flowing rivers. As we and the light got nearer, details began to emerge from the gloom.

There was a gate across the island, barring the entrance to a small one-story building. It was a dirty, tired looking hut, built of worn and ancient stone that had discolored. The roof barely clung to the walls and looked to be made of straw or mud. The gate however... The gate was gleaming. Made of criss-crossed iron bars, it looked like something you'd see outside a fifth avenue apartment block, grand and imposing. The green light bobbed towards it a couple times, then settled a few feet higher than the gate's peak. The chariot slowed and we all stared.

There were things tied to the iron bars. Hundreds of things, bits of old paper, cups, jewelry, rags, weapons, all sorts of stuff.

'Do you think the green gem is on there somewhere?' I whispered, the absence of the rushing wind now making it eerily silent.

A low rumbling growl met my words.

'If it is, go and look now, before...' Hecate trailed off as a dog twice the height of me emerged from the darkness, stepping out of the iron gate like it was some sort of portal. He looked a bit like a greyhound, if a greyhound was jet black, blessed with too many teeth and had a tail made from fire.

I gulped.

'Olethros,' whispered Hecate.

'Remind me what that means?'

'Destruction.'

'Excellent.'

Olethros barked once, and the flames from his tail streaked across his lithe body, lighting spirals of fire that danced over his sleek fur.

'Why is everything in this fucking hellhole on fire?'

'Go, Persephone,' said Morpheus. 'We must not forget we are in a race.'

'That's easy for you to say,' I muttered, as my vines snaked from my palms, my gaze still fixed on the dog now prowling up and down the length of the gate. 'How the hell do I get past him?'

'We can't help you, Persy.'

'Right.'

I took a big breath, and whipped my vine toward the rocky island, far from the iron gate. Olethros froze, his black eyes fixing on my flickering vine. 'Come on, doggy,' I coaxed. 'Take the bait.' He lowered on his huge haunches, his ears flattening against his head. 'That's it...'

He pounced, and dammit, he was so quick I didn't have time to whip the vine out of the way. His long snout closed over the vine, but not hard enough to sever it, and he jerked his head. With a yelp, I was pulled from the chariot.

I had a split second to react, before I would slam into the ground at the hound's feet, and I threw my other hand out, shooting a vine desperately at the iron gate. It caught and coiled around the iron bars just in time, my body bouncing like it was on a bungee-cord between the twelve-foot-tall dog and the massive gates. Olethros shook his enormous head and I bit back a cry as my shoulder was wrenched hard from its socket. I willed the vine the dog had hold of to disintegrate, then shortened the other, pulling myself fast towards the gate whilst sending my healing power to my shoulder.

But now I was a moving target, and Olethros snarled as he raced after me. I crashed into the gate and wasted no time scrambling up it, each diamond-shaped gap between the bars as long as my legs and difficult to pull myself up. I sent my vines from my palms ahead of me, helping to drag myself higher and making sure that if I fell I wouldn't fall far. I felt Olethros smash into the gate a second later, the whole structure shaking hard. My heart was hammering against my ribs, but adrenaline had caused my focus to sharpen, and I was scanning every bit of junk I was passing as I climbed higher.

After what felt like an eternity I cast a glance down, checking I was out of the hound's reach, before slowing to a stop. He was jumping, snapping at me, giving big echoing barks that made my head hurt. But he couldn't reach me. I took a second to get my breath back, then looked along the gates, desperately seeking out anything green. Knowing the asshole gods, they would have put the thing I needed to get low down, well within the dog's reach. The spirals of fire covering Olethros were getting bigger and unease rippled through me. He would be completely on fire soon.

But then the fire-light from his body reflected off something bright and colorful, and my eyes widened as they fixed on the object. A pendant, tied to the iron gate only ten feet off the ground, set with a massive grass-green gem.

Reaching to my left, I awkwardly untied the nearest thing to me with one hand, which was a warrior helmet, complete with faded red plume. As soon as the cord came loose it fell, and I sent silent thanks into the gloom as it clattered to the ground, drawing the dog's attention immediately. His ears pricked as the clattering continued, and I couldn't help giving a fist pump as the helmet began to roll noisily away from the gate. Olethros followed.

I didn't waste a second. Using my vine to control my descent, I launched myself from the gate to the ground, then ran to where the pendant was. I scrambled the few feet up the gate as quietly as I could, holding my breath as I reached the gem and frantically started to pull at the cord. I heard a growl in the distance, and my sweating hands fumbled with the knots. I couldn't untie the damned thing. I needed something to cut it.

'You're an idiot,' I cursed myself as pulled *Faesforos*

from its sheath and sliced through the cord like it was nothing. The pendant dropped to the ground before I could catch it, and I jumped from the gate after it. I crouched to grab it, elation surging through me as I put it safely around my neck, then straightened. My heart skipped a beat.

Olethros was bounding towards me and he looked pissed. I tipped my head back, finding the chariot above me, and threw both palms out towards it, praying like hell that one of them would catch. Almost as the hound reached me, I felt resistance on one of them and pulled. I shot upward, but Olethros was fast. He jumped at the same time, snapping at my leg, his razor sharp teeth tearing through the muscle of my right calf. I screamed as white-hot pain raced up my leg, and my skin went tight and cold over my whole body. Dizziness swamped me as I kept rising, then there were hands pulling at my shoulders. Hecate was dragging me onto the chariot, the small space barely big enough for me to sit.

'Heal yourself, quickly. That bite will turn nasty fast,' she said urgently. I concentrated, trying to block out the searing pain and drawing my healing power to my leg. Warmth replaced the tight icy feeling, then soothing magic tingled over the wound, spreading throughout my body. My magic was removing the toxins I knew were spreading from the bite.

'I think it's working,' I panted.

'Good,' she answered, and her grip on my shoulder relaxed. I felt strength returning to my limbs, the tightness in my chest easing and the dizziness receding. Last

time I had been poisoned I couldn't heal myself. Now...
Now I was strong. Strong enough to fix myself. *Strong
enough to fix Hades.*

'Let's go, Morpheus,' I said loudly, getting slowly to my
feet. I wobbled, but Hecate and the side of the chariot
kept me upright.

'You got it,' he said, and the chariot took off after the
little green light, into the darkness.

TWENTY-TWO

PERSEPHONE

W e chased the green light out of the mountain and found ourselves flying through a high-sided gulley, the Styx and the Acheron flowing side-by-side below us.

'Incoming!' called Morpheus, and I squinted to see the red light fast approaching, Minthe's chariot behind it.

She was on her way to Olethros, which meant she had her first gem too. Shit.

My vines sprang from my palms, ready, and Hecate raised her hands, her eyes turning milky, as the red chariot got closer.

The lights neared each other, forcing our chariots within striking distance of one another. The flails on the side of ours leaped to life, whirling fast on their chains, stretching beyond the spikes. But the red bags on the end on the ropes on Minthe's chariot rose too, and as a crossbow bolt whizzed by my head, the mountains around us rumbled. Minthe's eyes caught mine as she raised her arms, and rocks exploded from the bags. I threw myself down, below the side of the chariot, yelling for Morpheus to do the same. He did, as a wall of blue light burst from Hecate, stopping about half of the rain of sharp stones from landing in the chariot. But the rest got through, and the chariot began to tip forward in a nose dive toward the ground.

'Morpheus!' I shrieked, and the chariot leveled sharply, tipping me onto my ass. My heart leaped into my mouth as I lost my grip, but my vines instinctively coiled around the wooden edge of the chariot and steadied me.

'They're past,' called Hecate, and I got quickly to my feet.

'Are you hurt?' I asked as Morpheus pushed himself up.

'A little,' he said, and a trickle of blood that shone a weird silver color ran down his temple. 'But it'll heal. I need to concentrate.'

'OK,' I said, and turned to watch Minthe's chariot get smaller as they approached Olethros' cave. 'Well, I'd say they won that encounter.'

Morpheus did a perfect job of weaving between the geysers of glowing liquid that the rivers shot up at us as we raced after the green light, and eventually we moved up out of the ravine. My breath caught as wind rushed over us, the view of the sprawling rock landscape covered in glowing streams truly magnificent in its own other-worldly way.

The green light darted off toward another steep incline, and we zipped after it, until it reached a long, flattened ledge in the rock. It slowed abruptly, and my pulse quickened. Had we reached the second dog?

'Fonax is the ancient word for bloodthirsty, Persy, you need to be really careful. He doesn't look as bad as Olethros, but trust me, he's worse.' I nodded at Hecate as we moved lower, toward the ledge.

'If Minthe could handle him, so can I,' I said determinedly.

But when Fonax came into view, pacing the ledge with predatory grace, my insides skittered. He was a smoky gray color, broad, and much smaller than the last hound, probably waist high on me. He paused, sniffing the air as we neared him and I noticed that his short snout was dripping with something red, and his eyes were gleaming scarlet. Then he growled deep in his throat, and I saw his blood red teeth as he bared them in our direction.

'What do you mean, he doesn't look as bad as Olethros? He looks just as bad!' I exclaimed.

'He's smaller, and not on fire,' she protested.

'He has red eyes and teeth. That's pretty fucking creepy.'

'This is a race, ladies,' called Morpheus, interrupting us. I clenched my jaw, and scanned for anything at all on the ledge that might be hiding a gem. I spotted a large iron ring on the ground, and could just make out what looked like a trapdoor beneath it.

. . .

Deciding to deploy the same tactic as before, I asked Morpheus to get us as close to the trapdoor in the ledge as he safely could. Fonax started barking as we approached, and waves of icy fear slammed into me. Hades had said his dogs could instill fear in people, I remembered. But if they were like him, I could block it out with my power. I focused, using my healing magic to create a shield around my head, blocking the visions I knew would come if I didn't protect myself. Confident it was working, I snaked my vines out, then flung one as far from the trapdoor as I could.

Fonax raced after it, and I sent the vine from my right hand to the iron ring on the trapdoor. I held my breath as I jumped the ten feet from the chariot to the ground, and landed hard on one leg, failing to use my vine properly to slow the jump. I cried out as my ankle twisted and I fell. The shout was all Fonax needed to realize I'd tricked him. He spun, turning a hundred and eighty degrees in a heartbeat, and raced toward me. I yanked as hard as I could on the vine on the trapdoor, both trying to open it and pull myself to my feet. It creaked but didn't open, and I stumbled toward it, crying out again when I put weight on my left leg.

'Open! Fucking open!' I forced my power into the green vine, desperately pulling on it as the hound got closer, his gleaming red eyes terrifying.

With a lurch the trapdoor finally gave way, and I threw myself into the dark space without a moment's hesitation, tugging the door shut behind me with the vine. Nothing down there could be worse than Fonax reaching me. As the trapdoor closed above me it severed the vine that was attached, and I tumbled through the darkness until I landed on something relatively soft.

Panic rose in my chest as I rolled, struggling to right myself. I had no idea what I was on top of and the thought was nauseating.

Dirt. I moved my hands around hesitantly as I came to a stop on my ass, and was pretty sure I was sitting on piles of sandy dirt. I paused as my fingers skimmed something solid. I needed light. Cautiously, I sent a gold vine from my palm, hoping the glow it gave off would be enough to see by.

It was, just. I was in a small, dirt-filled space, the ceiling not much taller than I would be, standing up. I moved the vine down and saw that I had run my hand over a broken doll. As I looked, I saw more bits of junk, half buried in the sand. I immediately began to dig, searching for anything green in the dim golden light.

Another volley of barking began above me, making me jump in surprise, then a fierce scratching sound began. Fonax was trying to get through the trapdoor.

I dug faster, sending my power to my ankle to try to heal it. As soon as the power flowed to my leg, waves of fear crashed into me, flames and screams rushing into my mind. Corpses, the bodies of those I had killed... My hands stilled in the dirt as the scratching got louder, and sweat broke out across my forehead as terror began to claw its way up my chest.

I forced my healing magic back to my head, abandoning healing my ankle. Slowly the screams died away, and my pulse slowed slightly.

Breathing hard, I flexed my shaking hands, trying to block out the frantic scratching and barking. If my healing power could only protect me from the fear or heal my ankle, not both, then I would have to make do with my busted ankle. The fear would cripple me.

I rolled onto my knees, and resumed digging in the dirt, tossing ancient crap out of the way, and seeing nothing green.

The scratching overhead stopped abruptly, and an ominous creak replaced it. I paused, glancing up at where the trapdoor was. A resounding crack made me gasp in shock, then a slither of light streamed through the wood.

'Shit,' I said, and turned back to the dirt, moving as fast as I could on my hands and knees, my glowing vine close to the ground. 'Come on, come on, come on,' I muttered frantically, trying to ignore the thought that was repeating itself over and over in my head.

Even if I found the damned gem, I had no fucking idea how to get back out of the trapdoor and past the hound.

By the time the time I found the green stone, embedded in a ring barely big enough to fit on my finger, most of the trapdoor was in shreds. I staggered to my feet as I shoved the ring on my pointer finger, my ankle wobbly and sore, but not agonizing. Sweat was rolling down my back, and my mind racing with bad ideas. I had no way of getting past Fonax and out of this space. Claustrophobia added to my growing panic, the low ceiling and dark gloom closing in on me.

A crack louder than any of the previous drew my attention to the trapdoor, and my heart almost stopped in my chest as a large piece of wood dropped into the space, followed immediately by Fonax.

He was glowing, the same red as his eyes and teeth. His ears were back, his shoulders hunched, and his lethal gaze fixed on me.

'H-h-h-hello,' I stuttered, holding my hands out. 'Who's a good boy?' I said. He snarled, dark liquid dripping from his teeth. I tried to reach out with my mind, like I did to talk to Skop, but there was nothing there. 'You don't want to eat me, Fonax. Your master will be super pissed with you if you do that,' I whispered, as the hound stalked closer. My gold vines were turning black as they swirled about me, preparing for a fight.

Fonax pounced. Fortunately for me he couldn't get much height in the cramped space, and my vines hit him square in the chest. I wasn't filled with enough hatred or anger for them to go through him, like they had Eurynomos, but they knocked him off course, and began to coil around his front legs and chest. He snarled and growled as he fought to get free of them, his powerful body pushing me backward in the dirt as I fought to cling on.

He stopped fighting for a split second, then seemed to throw everything he had into lunging for me. My vines only just held him back as his teeth snapped at my midriff.

'Oh no you don't,' I said, and felt his power start to flow down the vines, into me. Dark black tattoos began to spread across his fur, and he yelped and struggled. Unlike before, when I'd used my black vines, I seemed to have more control over the flow of power. I wasn't immediately rushed by the hell-hound's dark energy. 'I'm sorry, Fonax, but I have to win this,' I told him, edging my way around him, toward the trapdoor. 'I'm just going to take enough of your power that I can escape.'

But as the dog's bloodthirsty energy flowed into me, the more I felt like taking all of it. I would need it after all, to get past Cerberus. More power couldn't be a bad thing, could it? I felt Fonax stop fighting, and looked into his angry red eyes.

No. That was the Underworld talking, not me. I didn't need his dark, vicious power. I had my own.

Slowly, I released one vine, whipping it back to me and sending it up, out of the trapdoor. I felt it coil round something solid, a rock, I guessed, and tugged on it. It held. 'I'm going to leave now,' I said, feeling powerful. I felt like I could conquer the world, let alone one dog.

Kill. Blood, death, kill.

The words ricocheted through my skull, and I shook my head. *That's Fonax, the bloodthirsty hell-hound, not you,* I told myself firmly.

'Stay there,' I said aloud, and let the other vine disintegrate. He didn't have enough power to come after me, I was sure.

I was wrong. The second my vine vanished, he went for me, closing the gap between us in a heartbeat. His jaws clamped onto my thigh and I screamed, the same white-hot pain I'd felt from Olethros searing through me. I yanked on the vine, and my feet left the floor, tearing my leg from Fonax's mouth, and leaving a chunk of my flesh between his jaws.

Rage blurred my vision, the voice in my head now louder than my own thoughts.

Kill! Burn! Blood!

I burst up through the hole where the trapdoor had been, my vine dragging me along the rocks, the pain interrupting the fury flooding through me.

'Persy!' yelled Hecate, and I rolled to see the chariot just a few feet from me, by the ledge.

But I didn't want to get back on the chariot. Now I had a score to settle, with an ungrateful, murderous hell-hound. I pushed myself onto my knees, dimly aware of the massive amount of blood pouring from my thigh. 'Persy, stop the bleeding, now!'

I ignored her, crawling back towards the trapdoor.

'Persephone, what are you doing? Get back on the chariot!' Morpheus shouted. But fury had taken over, Fonax's bloodthirsty Underworld magic coursing through my body.

'Persy, if you don't stop the bleeding, you will die, and

Hades needs you!' Hecate's words finally pierced the fog. *Hades*. Hades and Minthe and... The race. The Trials.

I turned, the pain penetrating through the rage, obliterating all other thoughts. *Heal*. I had to heal myself. Fonax was trapped in the space under the trapdoor, and I'd taken most of his power, so when I sent my magic at my leg, no crippling torrents of fear hit me. Slowly, painfully, the wound began to close.

'Persephone, you have to get back on the chariot, we can't lose this much time,' Morpheus said, his voice calmer. I looked sideways, my head swimming, and saw that he had pulled the chariot up alongside the ledge.

'OK,' I stammered, dragging myself up onto my feet. I limped to the ledge, each step agony, still sending as much power as I could to my thigh, and Hecate pulled me onto the wood.

'Tell me you got the gem,' she said, wincing at my leg as I propped my back against the side of the chariot. I felt it lurch into motion as I held up my hand to her, showing her the ring.

'Yeah. I got the gem.'

TWENTY-THREE

HADES

'Let me go!' I roared, for the hundredth time. Ankhiale rolled her eyes at me, just as she had every other time.

'Good gods, you're irritating. If you're careless enough to let me trap you, then you should handle the consequences like a real man.'

I glared down at the metal band glowing around my wrist, furious that she'd managed to get it there. If I'd known she'd had it I would have fought differently.

'I know who gave this to you,' I hissed. It was a manacle forged by Hephaestus, and there were only three in existence. They were able to bind a god of almost any strength, and due to their exceptional power were only ever used in extreme circumstances.

And the only gods they were entrusted to were the three strongest; Zeus, Poseidon and myself.

I shook my wrist, pouring the little power I could still access into the metal, but the manacle didn't move. It was chained to an iron stake in the ground, pinning me in place. I knew it was useless. I used my own manacle to transport powerful prisoners to Tartarus, until it was no longer needed to trap them and limit their power. I knew how unbreakable the magic was. And I knew that only one of my brothers could remove it.

'Well yeah, it's pretty fucking obvious,' Ankhiale said, stepping through the ring of flames she'd created around me. I couldn't survive her fire without my power. My mind was racing, fear for Persephone overruling all else. I was useless here. 'That pathetic water-loving brother of yours isn't strong enough to free a Titan from Tartarus,' Ankhiale smiled at me.

She was right. Poseidon would never have enough dominion in the Underworld. But Zeus...

'He orchestrated the Trials here so that I would have to relinquish control of the Underworld to him. It was nothing to do with finding me a wife. It's why he found Persephone.'

She nodded, her flaming hair falling about her face, her blood red lips pulled up in a grin.

'The longer the Trials have gone on, and the more control you have allowed him, the more power he has gained here. He's the strongest of all of you. All he needed was a little time, and a little deference from you. And the girl.'

'I *am* the Underworld,' I spat. 'He can not beat me in my own realm.' She chuckled.

'It would appear he already has, little Lord,' she said, gesturing at my wrist. I instinctively drew on my power, but the response was just a pathetic swell of fury, coursing uselessly through me. I couldn't channel it into magic, no matter how hard I tried.

'Why would Zeus free you? He hates you, and all other Titans.' I couldn't make sense of it. The very last Olympian who would want Cronos to be free was Zeus, surely?

'Ego and hatred are powerful emotions, Hades. The world has forgotten how evil we Titans are supposed to be. They are allowed into the academies to learn magic alongside the other citizens, they are allowed to work and live in the realms, treated the same as everyone else. And now, to top it off, you've given one of our most powerful, the mighty Oceanus, his own realm in Olympus.' I stared at her in disbelief.

'You're saying Zeus is freeing Cronos to show the world that Titans are bad?'

'He doesn't think Cronos will actually make it to freedom. He thinks he can use me, and your lovely ex-wife, to let Cronos wreak a touch of havoc, reminding the world of what Titans are capable of, before he swoops in and saves the day. And then all will hail our mighty King Zeus.' She gave a mocking bow. 'But he's a fucking fool,' she hissed straightening suddenly. 'As soon as Cronos gets his hands on that little flower goddess of yours, Zeus will not be able to contain him. Nobody will!'

TWENTY-FOUR

PERSEPHONE

Morpheus kept us on course as we raced along the Styx, to the gates of the Underworld and Cerberus. My leg was still stiff, but the wound was completely closed now, and any loss of blood I may have experienced was being offset by the power still coursing through me from Fonax. I was keeping the voice commanding me to kill at bay by clinging to the image of Hades' face, but the more I thought about him, the more intense his fear felt through the bond, which in turn was making me more anxious and angry and susceptible to the dark power.

'Please tell me we're almost there,' I yelled over the rushing wind.

'Over there,' shouted Hecate, and pointed. We were making our way over ground that was gradually sloping upward and I could just make out a dark hole in the rock above us, that the glowing blue river seemed to be streaming from.

It only took a few moments more to reach it, and I flexed my fists as we entered the darkness.

We flew into a long cavern, and my jaw fell open as I stared around myself. The river veered off to the right, immediately obscured from view by the walls of the cavern. But the walls weren't made from rock, they were made from *wings*. A hundred feet tall and the same again in length, they stretched the length of the cavern, struts that looked like ribs holding them up at intervals. They were slightly transparent, and I could see huge flames flickering behind then, casting everything in a fiery orange glow. We slowed as we flew further into the long hall, and I saw what the wings were attached to. At the end of the room was a huge iron gate with thick bars, and towering above it, a statue of a demon, the wing walls curving from its back. It looked like a grotesque gargoyle, with fangs and horns and sagging stone skin and I shuddered.

'Wow,' I breathed. The gates of hell were terrifying. Impressive, but terrifying. 'Where's Cerberus?' I asked. The second the dog's name left my lips, a rumbling growl began to roll through the air. Morpheus brought the chariot to a stop, just a few feet above the ground.

'I don't know, but here's Minthe,' muttered Hecate, looking behind us. Her red chariot was pelting toward us, and as she neared I saw that her arm was wrapped in fabric, blood seeping through the material. She couldn't heal, I remembered, and Olethros' bite was toxic.

'Are you alright?' I called to her, as they slowed. Sanape growled and leveled her crossbow at me, but Minthe barked something at her.

'Fine,' she shouted back at me. 'May the best woman win!'

I nodded at her, as respectfully as I could, and turned back to Hecate, who was giving me a strange look.

'You do actually want to win this, right?'

'Yeah, but not by letting someone else die,' I snapped.

'Her health is not your problem. It's extremely good for you that she's injured.' A loud snarl cut across her words, and all the hairs on my skin stood on end.

'I'll win because I deserve to, not because she dies,' I said quietly, vines snaking from my palms. 'Where's Cerberus?' I asked again, before she could say anything else on the subject.

'He doesn't normally guard the inside of the gates,' she said. 'Persy, if you get bitten by him, you're not going to have long to fix it. His power over fear is as strong as Hades' is, and that almost killed you once.'

'OK,' I nodded. 'I won't let him bite me.' My stomach clenched in anxiety, and I flexed my fingers, my vines turning black. 'I'm ready.'

As if on cue, a creature melted through the iron gates, and I felt my knees go weak.

He was a combination of the other two hounds, in the worst possible way. Thirty feet tall, his dark body was covered in dancing flames. At his shoulders his neck split into three, and each broad, snarling head had angular eyes that looked like blood-red gemstones, and dark red liquid dripped from lethal fangs. Terror gripped my chest as I stared at the beast, fear spreading through my body all the way to my bones. Cerberus' ears pricked up, and all three heads barked. The sound rocked through me, and I clapped my hands over my ears as dread coursed through my veins. *Fire, flesh, blood...* I was drowning.

'Persy!' Hecate caught me as my legs buckled.

I snapped my magical shield up, and for a moment it did nothing. But then light broke through the dark spots in my eyes, the desire to run and run and run fading. My legs steadied, and Hades' face filled my mind, fierce and passionate. I was here for a reason, I couldn't run.

I had to win.

'Where's the gem?' I said, breathing hard. Morpheus pointed, and my insides clenched again. Glinting in the orange light, on a silver chain around Cerberus's middle head, were two gems the size of my fist. One green, and one red. I gaped, looking between Hecate and Morpheus.

'How the hell am I supposed to get onto his neck? He's on fucking fire!' They both stared back at me, Hecate's eyes filled with apology.

'We can't help you, Persy,' she said eventually.

'But Minthe has a plan, so you'd better come up with

something fast,' said Morpheus, and I spun to see the other chariot powering toward the giant dog.

There was no way I could land on top of him, I'd be burned instantly, I thought, trying to play out scenarios as fast as I could in my head. But from underneath him, perhaps I could use my vines to reach the silver chain collar.

'Take me down,' I asked Morpheus, and he nodded, the chariot immediately dropping to the rock. I wasted no time, sprinting toward Cerberus. He snarled as I approached, then his right head moved up sharply, snapping at Minthe's chariot. Taking advantage of the distraction, I threw myself to the ground and slid. One huge flaming head came down, fangs terrifying as they chomped at me, but I made it underneath his massive chest before he could reach me. He barked again, the sound so loud I thought my head might explode. I wriggled around on my back, looking up at the underside of his body as his clawed paws stamped around me. The flames didn't extend under his chest, and I saw a pendant on a chain that was stretched over his barrel shaped ribs, bouncing against his black fur. Squinting, I made out the image of a skull, with a rose wrapped around it. Without thinking, I leaped into a crouch and jumped for the pendant. The second my hand closed around it, Cerberus howled.

It was so much worse than his bark. The sound instilled a terror that I had simply never felt in my life, waves of fear beating against my shield, impulses to run and hide and cry pulsing through my mind as I fought them.

After what seemed like an age, the howling mercifully stopped. Gasping, I inched forward, trying to get under his heads to see the collar, and I realized with a start that he was no longer on fire.

The pendant... Had it somehow stopped the fire? Mind racing, I changed course, running instead for his tail. If he wasn't on fire, I could climb up his back.

But so could Minthe.

As I emerged from underneath him, I twisted, launching my vines at the base of his tail and pulling myself up fast. His left head turned, snapping at his rear end, but he couldn't reach me as I landed at the base of his tail. My stomach twisted as I looked up and saw Minthe, wrapped tight around the neck of his right head. Tears streaked her pretty face as the head thrashed, and blood still seeped through her bandage. But she was closer to the collar than I was. And I had to win this.

Focusing on the central head, I ran up Cerberus' enormous spine, my arms flailing either side of me like a damned tightrope walker. The only thing that kept me upright as the dog stamped around was my speed. I threw myself at the middle neck as my foot finally slipped, but I missed. I fired my vines as I slid, and one coiled around Cerberus's neck, catching me as my body followed my foot, dangling between his middle and left heads. The third head snapped and snarled, and I swung myself desperately out of the way. I could see the gems glinting on the collar, high above me. But then I saw Minthe, her head appearing over the top of his central neck, gripping the chain collar. She saw my vine and paused, her gaze following it to where I was dangling. Her hand appeared by her head, a knife in it. *She was going to cut the vine.* I sent another one up fast, and it coiled around the collar. A blast of hot breath was my only warning that the third head was coming in for another go at eating me, and I pulled on both vines hard, willing them to shorten. The giant jaws missed me by inches. Cerberus howled again, and I winced, pain and a feeling of utter hopelessness lancing though my head.

I only had seconds before Minthe reached her gem. But she hadn't cut my vine. I looked up at her as I grabbed for the underside of the collar, and saw that she had one arm wrapped across her face, the other clinging to the top of the collar. I was only a few feet from her now.

I scrabbled at the collar, trying to twist it to reach the green gem, but it was thicker than my arm and wouldn't budge. The left head chomped at where Minthe was and I heard her whimper. She couldn't block out the fear like I could.

I yanked on the chain, pulling myself up and around the other side of his neck, closer to the gem. The right head swooped at me, and I launched a black vine at it, adrenaline powering through me.

I was so close.

The vine collided with Cerberus' temple, then began to coil around his ear. I couldn't make the dog weak by draining his power, or Minthe would have a chance too.

The only reason she hadn't already got her gem was the fear crippling her. But I could at least keep one of the heads distracted. Cerberus shook his head violently, trying to dislodge my vine and making me wobble, but I held on. Using my legs I hauled myself up next to Minthe. She was trembling but her breathing was slowing.

'Do you really love him?' I heard her say, her voice weak. I froze.

'Yes.'

The left head barked suddenly, twisting toward us. I moved fast, lunging for the green gem. My fingers closed around it, and I pulled.

TWENTY-FIVE

PERSEPHONE

Blue light flashed all around us, and suddenly Cerberus was shrinking. Minthe yelped at the same time I cried out, then the chariot was right next to me, and Morpheus was yanking me onto it.

'Well done!' he yelled, as I fell on my butt on the wood.

'What's happening? Did I win?' Light was flashing around me like a strobe, totally disorientating me. I blinked down at my hand, the green gem huge and glowing. Had I done it? Had I really won?

But we were moving.

'Morpheus, where are we-' I cut off as I turned, confusion turning fast to fear. 'Where's Hecate?' Morpheus was facing ahead, and as the flashing lights lessened, I realized that we were speeding out of the orange glowing cavern.

I sprang to my feet, dropping the gem and gripping the chariot edge. 'Morpheus!' I yelled, wind rushing over me as we burst back out over the rocky landscape, the glowing rivers snaking across the Underworld below us. 'Morpheus, what's going on?' Black vines pushed out of my palms.

'You'll see in a moment,' he yelled back, without turning to me.

'See what? Where's Hecate?'

'This was her idea! But she'll be punished worse than I will, so we agreed I'd take you alone.'

'Take me where?'

'The river Lethe.'

This was wrong. Every tense muscle in my body was screaming at me as I reached out desperately in my mind for Hades or Hecate, but nobody responded.

I'd spent so much of my time here trying to work out how to get my memories back, but not like this. I'd just got the gem from Cerberus, I'd just won the damned Hades Trials, I should be celebrating with Hades, not flying to the one place I wasn't supposed to go!

'Morpheus, I want to go back. I want to see Hades.' I tried to keep my voice level, but it came out strained.

'You've come too far, Persephone. You must see this through.'

'Why are you doing this? I want to talk to Hecate.'

'I told you, she's holding back the others, this was her idea.'

'I don't believe you.' And I didn't. Hecate would not spring something like this on me. She loved Hades, and if

Hades said I wasn't to get my memories back, then Hecate would support him.

We were swooping low through a gully, flying over the purple river, and a glimpse of sunshine yellow caught my eye in the distance. The river Lethe.

'You can't make me do this,' I said.

'I don't want to make you do anything. I'm trying to help you.' I thought about using my vines, but if he crashed the chariot we would both die, and I had no idea how to control it if I managed to disable him. It would be safer to get away once we were on the ground. I reached out desperately with my mind again for Hades or Hecate, but there was nothing.

As soon as the chariot touched down on the rocks on the bank of the yellow river, I launched my vines at Morpheus, but he spun to me, the air in front of him shimmering and bending and an image coming into view. My vines fell to the floor as I recognized my brother's face, a sleepy expression across it.

'Sam?' I realized I was looking at the Judgment Hall, but the crowds were gone, only my brother and Skop remaining. Skop was in naked gnome form, and he looked equally as out of it. 'What's happening?' I demanded. Hedone stepped into the image, a sad look on her face.

'This is a portal, like the flame dishes. One of my godly gifts,' said Morpheus. 'Hedone's gift is bewitching those around her with her irresistible charm. Men like your brother and Skop are particularly susceptible.'

Anger surged through me, and my vines whipped up again.

'I thought you were my friends!'

'I'm sorry, Persy, but our cause is bigger than any of us individually. It has to be this way,' said Hedone, through the portal. She looked genuinely sad and I blinked at her.

'What cause? Why are you doing this?'

'The gods need to be taught a lesson. They need to know that they can't treat mortals like toys, wipe their memories, force them into action for their own entertainment.' Hedone's voice became hard as she spoke.

'What's that got to do with me? And where's Hecate?' Hedone pointed and the portal swung, showing Hecate's prostrate body on the marble.

'Hecate!' I yelled, and the portal swung back.

'She is only unconscious,' said Morpheus. 'At this stage we have no reason to kill her.' Fury was bubbling through me now, the remnants of Fonax's Underworld power surging through my veins.

'Kill her? I can't believe this! You were supposed to be my friends! Hecate's friends!' The betrayal stung to my core, and was making my eyes fill with tears, but I couldn't let them fall. I couldn't look weak. They had my real friends, and my brother.

'It wasn't supposed to play out like this,' Morpheus said. 'It was supposed to be simple, but so many things have gone wrong.' There was a bitter edge to his voice. 'Hedone implanted the memory of what you did in the humans so that they could scare you into getting your power back, but she lost control of one and he showed up with the phoenix at the ball. So, we changed tactics. But Hades got to you in Tartarus before Cronos could when we sent you there before.' I felt like ice was trickling down my spine, my head pounding with anger and shock.

'Why? Why are you doing this?'

'That is why we are here, at the river Lethe. Cronos and Hedone believe that you will be more cooperative if you know the truth. You will understand then why we must do what we are doing, the magnitude of our task.' His eyes were wide, and his skin was swirling with light as his words increased in volume. 'Drink. Drink from the river. Restore your memories.'

'No,' I said. For weeks I had yearned for my lost past, but not like this. If my memories were linked with Cronos and these maniacs, then Hades was right, I wanted nothing to do with them.

Morpheus sighed.

'Hedone, my sweet,' he said. Hedone moved, a long dagger appearing in her hand from the folds of her dress. Her eyes were filled with apology as she handed it to Sam. Horror filled me as my brother gazed at the blade.

'Sam, my love, place the tip of the dagger on your chest for me? You'd make me so very happy,' she beamed at him, her voice like honey. Sam smiled stupidly at her as he lifted the blade to his chest. 'Now when I say push, you must push. It won't hurt, it will feel like bliss.' Sam's smile widened.

'No!' I screamed, as I stepped towards the portal, flinging my vine towards the dagger. But the image just shimmered as my vine passed harmlessly through it. My heart hammered so hard against my ribs I thought it might burst free, and I felt sick as the hot tears finally spilled down my cheeks. I looked at Morpheus, hopeless dread gripping my body. I couldn't get to Sam to save him.

'Drink, Persephone,' he said. 'Now.'

I knelt slowly next to the river, my mind racing. Would Hedone really kill Sam? She didn't look like she'd wanted to, but her voice when she had spoken to him had been as smooth as silk, laced with seduction. Not a hesitation or wobble. I couldn't take the risk. I reached down, cupping my hands and dipping them into the glowing sunshine-yellow liquid. A rush of memories blasted through me, memories of mom holding me as I cried, memories of Sam helping me pick up books in the corridors at school. Memories of Professor Hetz and the botanical gardens, and of my apartment.

I took a shuddering breath as I lifted my hands out of the river, water dripping slowly from the bowl my palms had formed.

'I don't want to do this,' I tried one more time, as I looked up at Morpheus. He shook his head slowly at me.

'This is out of our hands, Persephone. It is bigger than you or I. Drink.'

Gooseflesh covered my skin as I closed my eyes and lifted my cupped hands to my face, and drank.

'Persephone, how can you possibly be a better queen to Hades if you don't even know the Underworld properly?' I blinked at the voice, spinning around on the spot fast. I was in a dining room that looked a lot like the breakfast room in Hades' palace. I froze as I saw myself, sitting at a table with a man whose face I could not see. It was not Hades, that much I was sure of. I was wearing a black corseted dress, and my hair was as white as it was now, but I looked younger.

'I've made friends with the hounds now! And I've seen most of Virgo. Just not the really nasty bits,' the me who was sitting at the table told the man.

'If you truly want to help Hades, it's the worst parts of his world that you need to understand the most,' the man said. His voice was familiar, and I stepped closer cautiously.

'That does make sense,' younger me said slowly. 'You know, I have asked him to take me to Tartarus. But he always says no.'

'You're a Queen, Persephone. You have your own mind. And in my experience, it's always better to ask for forgiveness than permission.' The arrogant mischief in his voice finally clicked into place, and I let out a breath as I rounded the table.

Zeus.

He didn't look much like he did now, but his purple eyes were unmistakable.

'I suppose you're right,' younger me said, voice filled

with juvenile excitement. 'If you think it means I can help Hades rule better, I should do it. He'll understand. I'll take Cerberus with me, just in case.'

The image before me swirled and with a jolt, I was standing at the cave mouth before Tartarus, the flaming river burning beside me. Younger me was cocking her head at the inky blackness, and beside her was Cerberus, ten feet tall and swirling fiery spirals dancing over his fur. All three heads looked at younger me, then the closest nudged at her shoulder before turning, trying to walk away from the cave. Cerberus didn't want me to go in.

'Don't be silly. I'm Queen of the Underworld, everyone in there has to do as I say,' younger me said to the dog. Cerberus whined, but turned back to the cave. His tail drooped.

The scene before me whirled again, and I was in Tartarus. Ixion turned on his flaming wheel above us, and I stared as younger-me stood before a swirling mass of light and shadow. Cerberus was growling, deep and fearsome, but a voice drowned him out.

'I promise you, my Queen, I have been falsely judged. Zeus, Lord of the Gods himself, made sure that Hades was tricked and I was sent here for eternity. I am a god of light, and being trapped here in the dark is a torment too awful to endure.'

Nausea rolled through me. I recognized the voice. It was the stranger from the Atlas garden.

'Why should I believe you?' asked younger me, and the mass of light pulsed brightly.

'Because I speak the truth. I swear it.'

'Hmmm. You know, I can find out myself.' Slowly, younger-me lifted her hands, and vines snaked out of them. 'I can taste your power, find out exactly what sort of god you are,' she said, confidently.

'No,' I whispered. The vines turned black as they reached the mass, and a wave of power rippled through the deep red cavern. Younger-me gasped, dropping to her knees, and Cerberus howled, long and loud. The mass pulsed brighter, and the voice spoke again.

'You can take my power, but you can't contain it!' The words were spoken as a delighted realization, and a moan escaped younger-me's lips. Then a burst of bright blue illuminated the whole cavern, and a column of pure, blazing power smashed into the mass, tearing the vines from it. Hades, smoky and blue and enormous, scooped up younger me, and the scene flashed once again.

'It's too much,' younger me cried in Hades' arms. We were in a tiny rock room, barely any light around us.

'Let it out. It's safe down here, we're deep under the ground,' Hades said, his face a mask of pain.

'I can't. I can't. If I let go, his power will be free.'

'No, you only took a little. Let it go now, before it kills you.'

At his words, younger-me's body began to glow a deep blood red and with an agonized cry, waves of power burst from her skin. They smashed into the rock, and I saw the fear cross Hades' face as the walls began to crumble. He tightened his grip and flashed again, and then we were hovering in the sky above the ocean, islands dotting the blue.

I was looking at the realms of Olympus. He flashed again, and we were lower, looking over a series of small domes that were floating on the surface. They looked like the domes of Aquarius, but above the surface of the water instead of below.

Bile rose in my throat as rock burst from the waves, less than a mile from one of the domes. It grew and grew, and a whimper escaped me as I realized what it was. Red and black bubbled at the rock's peak, then a deafening boom echoed through the air.

It was a volcano.

Hades' face was white as he hovered in the sky, waves of red energy still pulsing from the body of my younger self, clutched in his arms. Lava spewed from the volcano, and I felt weak as I watched it rain over the nearest three domes. Tears flooded from my eyes as the screams began, and as desperately as I wanted to turn away, I couldn't. People fell as they ran through the streets, the fiery liquid chasing them down before they stood a chance of escaping. Buildings crashed to the ground as the lava melted them, crushing fleeing people.

A new scream pierced my ears, and I tore my eyes from the domes to see my younger self shrieking in

Hades' grip. The waves of red power had stopped and her gaze, *my gaze,* was transfixed on the fiery death and destruction below.

'Let me help, we have to help!' she was screaming, and I choked on a sob.

This is what I had done. I'd caused a volcano, and the death of hundreds of innocent people.

TWENTY-SIX

PERSEPHONE

The scene flashed again, and mercifully I wasn't taken down to the domes. I was back on the banks of the river Lethe, Morpheus towering over my crouched figure.

'Three of the domes above the surface were destroyed, and two below were cracked and flooded when the volcano rose from the sea bed,' said Morpheus, his voice gentle.

A strangled sound escaped my throat and more burning tears blurred my vision. Bile was burning my throat.

'I killed them. That's why Poseidon hates me.'

'You are not responsible for their deaths. Zeus is. He sent you down there, hoping you would die.'

I blinked up at Morpheus. 'Why?'

'He hated to see Hades happy. Zeus' ego is over-inflated to the point of mania. You were making Hades strong, and he couldn't handle it.'

'How do you know all this?'

'Cronos. He saw it in you when you connected with him.'

'You've been letting him talk to me. In my dreams,' I said, clinging to the words, forcing out the terrible, terrible knowledge I now had. That I couldn't face.

'Yes. I can't free him myself, but I can give him some access to humans, via their dreams.'

'The Atlas garden. You created it.'

'No. Cronos did. He is not who the world makes him out to be. He is strong and beautiful and a far, far better ruler than Zeus. This is why you needed to know the truth.'

'But to free him, you need me to die,' I said, struggling to my feet.

'Yes. But now you understand why. Zeus will destroy Olympus, and everything good in it, to prove his power to the world.'

'I don't understand.' Urgent thoughts were beginning to batter through my grief and revulsion, and I clawed at them mentally, using them to stabilize my spinning emotions. 'Where is Hades?' He should be here. He would be able to feel my pain through the bond, he should be here. 'And how did you send me to Tartarus before? Only Hades can do that. He thought an Olympian was involved.'

'And he was right. I may be powerful, and a resident of Virgo, but even I can only talk to Cronos via my dreams. I can't enter Tartarus, much less send someone else there. But the most powerful god in Olympus can, once Hades relinquished some control to him.'

'What? But that makes no sense, why would-' Morpheus cut me off with a vicious laugh.

'Persephone, Zeus is a dangerous lunatic! His hatred for Titans is no longer shared, and the citizens of Olympus are starting to accept them. How better to remind the world of their evil than to let Cronos out? Zeus thinks he can step in and save the day, and the world will remember why they worship him. But he is mistaken. Cronos is far, far stronger than him. He has forgotten the war too quickly, his inflated opinion of himself now so deluded that reality and fantasy have merged. He approached me not long after you were banished, when I was worried about Hades. My king was a shadow of himself. Zeus asked me to keep an extra eye on Cronos, should Hades neglect to, and I agreed, hoping to support my king. And I discovered that Cronos was not who I thought he was. He was fair and wise and everything Zeus was not. So when Zeus asked me to help him with this new plan, I agreed, but because I want Cronos in Zeus' place. I told Cronos what Zeus has planned, and even now Zeus still believes I am working for him. His ego will not allow him to believe otherwise.'

Fear and disbelief were overriding everything else in my head as Morpheus spoke. *Zeus was behind this. The only god more powerful than Hades.*

'Where is Hades?'

'He's tied up with a friend at the moment. But don't worry, Cronos has a proposition for you.'

'Why are you doing this? What's in it for you?'

'Love for Olympus, Persephone. Zeus needs to be removed, for the good of the world. Hades may not have told you, but the Underworld is seeing crueler people every year, and they are a result of his twisted society. Cronos will make the world a better place. And you're about to meet him.'

Protesting was useless as Morpheus watched me climb back on the chariot. With Sam, Hecate and Skop at his mercy, he knew I would do as he asked.

But the rational part of my brain knew they would die anyway if Cronos got his power into me and I went off like a bomb. I had to do something, but no matter how desperately I scrabbled around for a solution, nothing came. If Zeus had the other gods distracted, or convinced nothing was wrong, and Hades was trapped somewhere, then nobody was coming for me. I was on my own.

I barely saw the Underworld flash by below us, my mind was so focused on trying to come up with a plan that didn't involve everyone I loved dying. But as the flaming river came into view, my pulse raced even faster, my stomach lurching as we began to descend.

'Ah. There's Hades,' said Morpheus, from the head of the chariot, and my insides seared hot as the bond fired and I leaned over the chariot.

A little way off from the cavern that led to Tartarus, on a barren, uneven piece of rock, was a flaming ring twenty feet across. And at its center, on his knees, was Hades. His face snapped up to mine and I almost lost my grip on the chariot, his emotion rocketed through me so hard.

He was scared. And furious.

I reached for him desperately in my mind, but I couldn't hear him, couldn't get to him. There was no blue light around him, and his black trident lay useless nearby. Something had stripped his power, I realized. As the chariot soared over him, Ankhiale stepped out of the fire. She tilted her head and gave me a little finger wave, and a roar of frustration escaped me.

He's immortal. They can trap him, but they can't kill him. I clung to the thought, repeating the words over and over as we descended, and Hades and the fire witch disappeared from view. Pain surged through my gut again, my emotions mingling with Hades' as we lost sight of each other.

Morpheus set the chariot down at the mouth of the cave that led to Tartarus, and turned to me.

'Off you go, my Queen. Cronos is expecting you.'

'Only Hades, and apparently now Zeus, can enter or leave Tartarus,' I said, refusing to move my feet.

'I think you'll find that the winner of the Hades Trials, and Hades' Queen-to-be, also has that privilege,' he smiled at me.

Shit. What the hell was I going to do? Adrenaline was racing through my body, focusing my mind and building my power inside me. Which was exactly what I didn't want. My power couldn't help me here. In fact, it would be what killed me and everyone else in Virgo. And if Cronos was as bad as history and Hades said he was, possibly the whole of Olympus.

'I shouldn't have eaten those fucking seeds!' I yelled, and Morpheus blinked at my outburst.

'It's too late for regrets, Persephone. You will be a martyr. The little goddess who saved the world from a maniac.'

'You're the fucking maniac.'

'Ah, I see now that the shock is wearing off, the attitude is surfacing,' he said. 'I recommend being more polite to King Cronos.'

'Hades is your king, you filthy traitor,' I snarled.

'Not for much longer. Now go.'

I stared at him, desperation and fury boiling over inside me, with no outlet. With a hiss, I shot my arm out, and slapped him as hard as I could across the face.

'You're a fucking disgrace to the Underworld,' I spat, then stamped off the chariot, onto the rock. I didn't turn back as I marched towards the cavern. I couldn't face seeing if he would punish my brother or friends for my behavior, but I hadn't been able to help myself.

The orange flames of the river cast flickering shadows over the walls of the cave, and I walked fast. The last time I had been here, Hades had succumbed to the monster, and was about to set foot in Tartarus and take out his fury on the worst of the Underworld.

Perhaps I should have let him. Perhaps he would

have killed Cronos. I knew in my gut that that wasn't possible though. Hades had described Cronos as primordial in strength. He was truly immortal, unable to be destroyed. Memories of when I was last in Tartarus swept through me, the utter darkness, the screaming tortured souls, the endless fear. Panic threatened to engulf me, blackness swimming across my vision, but I bared my teeth as I pulled the thought of Hades into my mind.

I had to be strong. I had to work out a way to escape this.

At the mouth of Tartarus, I paused, squeezing my eyes closed and praying. *Please don't let me through, please don't let me through.* But disappointment melted through me as my foot entered the darkness without a hitch. I took a shuddering breath, and stepped through completely. The darkness was as terrifying as I remembered it, but this time power surged hard through me, blocking the fear and the smells. I couldn't block the sounds of screaming though, as I walked carefully forward, alongside the flaming river. With a screech and a flash, Ixion appeared above me, shrieking. I gulped back my trepidation and took another stride forward. All I had now was myself, and I was not going to cower in fear. Cronos would meet the goddess I knew was inside me, not a naive girl or a terrified woman.

He would meet the goddamned Queen of the Underworld.

· · ·

'Cronos!' I bellowed, summoning every ounce of courage within me. The flames in the river roared up, and a deep rumbling shook the ground. Illuminated on my right suddenly was a row of grand chairs, and a man sitting on one of them cried out when he saw me.

'Help me, please,' he screamed, and I recoiled as I saw the remnants of flesh and blood stuck to the vacant chairs. The man and the chairs melted back into the darkness before I could say a word.

'Cronos, I'm here!' I yelled again. The rumbling grew louder, then the mass of light I'd seen in the memory from the river appeared before me. Shadows intertwined with the white light, spinning and turning in a mesmerizing dance.

'Little goddess,' Cronos said, and a man stepped out of the light.

He was so beautiful I gasped, my lungs not working properly for a heartbeat. His eyes and his hair and his eyebrows were made of what looked like pure daylight, and instead of being creepy, it was stunning. He held his hands out and light shone from them too.

'I will not free you,' I choked out, my eyes streaming in his brightness.

'I wish, so very much, that you did not have to die. I would have liked for you to rule beside me.' The calm, soothing voice I had come to trust in the Atlas garden washed over me, and I clung to my anger, refusing to let him addle my brain.

'I will not free you,' I repeated. 'You can't make me use my vines.'

'It really is such a great shame to lose one as beautiful as you. But needs must. And the world's needs are greater than our own.'

'You were imprisoned here for a reason, and you will stay here,' I said, wishing desperately that I could grow, like Hades and the others did. Standing before Cronos, I felt tiny, despite his physical body being barely larger than mine. His presence was immense, as though he was light itself, more element than being.

'Little goddess, I have an offer for you to consider. I have become fond of you, and I would rather do this with you willing. It will hurt less.' My hands shook as I stared at him. He wasn't scared of me. My words had no effect on him at all. What the fuck was I going to do?

'You can't make me use my vines,' I said again. 'If I have to fucking stand in front of you like this forever, I will.'

'If you cooperate with me, I will allow Hades to live, free of his obligation to the Underworld,' Cronos said. I froze. 'I will free his soul of this place, and he will finally live the life he has always craved.'

TWENTY-SEVEN

HADES

I had to get to her.

Cronos was the strongest being still in existence in Olympus, and only my power over Tartarus gave me dominion over him.

Persephone didn't stand a chance. Fury swept through me, my head pounding with pain.

'You'll pay for this, Ankhiale! When I've got my power back, you'll fucking pay!' I bellowed. She stepped from the flames, shaking her head.

'Hades, you won't get your powers back, you fucking moron. You'll be consumed by them instead.'

'What if I offer you a deal?' I tried, changing tactics. 'What if I give you more than he can?' She laughed.

'More than Cronos can? Please. You're half as strong as him. What could you possibly-' she cut off abruptly, screwing her face up as a small flash of light sparked behind her. I frowned, then struggled to my feet as a shimmering burgundy powder appeared from nowhere, showering her whole body. A slow, easy smile spread across her face, then she giggled. 'There's six of you,' she slurred, then slumped to the ground.

'What the-' I started, then squinted as a small, naked gnome ran towards me. 'Skop?'

'Hedone thought she'd charmed me, but despite her being hot as holy hell, I am immune to such powers,' he said, talking fast as he reached me. I thrust the manacle out to him, one desperate hope left in me.

'Get my trident into the keyhole,' I said urgently. The trident could only be wielded by me, so it should be enough to unlock the manacle.

'I pretended she was in control, but secretly told Dionysus everything. He couldn't send me into Tartarus with Persephone, so he sent me to you instead. Armed with wine powder, but it won't last long. Ankhiale will come round in five minutes.'

'Zeus is behind all this,' I told the kobaloi, as he dragged the Trident toward me. It must have weighted three times what he did, and his bearded face showed the strain. Energy was building inside me, hope coursing through my veins.

'Dionysus worked that out when I told him you weren't really with Persephone. Zeus took the other gods to Leo to *give you two some time alone.* I believe Dionysus and Poseidon are confronting him now.' He had dragged the Trident to my feet and I ducked into a crouch, scooping it up with one hand.

'Help me,' I said, and together we wrestled the end of the long weapon into the manacle. With a roar, I forced the trident into the metal, and with a loud crack, the cuff opened.

Power flooded my body, the monster rearing loud and white-hot inside me, screaming up my chest, ready to end anyone or anything that stood between me and my Queen.

TWENTY-EIGHT

PERSEPHONE

Cronos could free Hades. Free him of his eternal obligation and let him live as he truly wanted to. If I was going to die anyway, surely this was a deal worth making?

What if you can stop him though! Don't give in! The fighter inside me screamed. But my heart ached as I thought about Hades consumed by the darkness, the idea of him living trapped in Tartarus as a mindless machine of violence unbearable.

I barely felt the vines snake from my palms.

As though on magnets, they burst toward Cronos.

'Wait!' I shouted, but it was too late, it was as though I no longer had control of them. A slow smile spread across Cronos' face as they reached him, and the storm of light around him shimmered a dark orange.

'It appears you have made your choice, Persephone.'

'No! No I hadn't decided yet!'

'Your power responded to your heart, little goddess. You would do anything for him.'

My vines coiled around his arms, and I sent every ounce of power I had in my body into them to keep them green. As soon as they turned black, they would take his power. Sweat rolled down my back as I concentrated.

'But the thing is, I lied.' My eyes snapped to his. 'Hades has been my keeper for a very, very long time. Do you really think I would not repay him for his actions? After you have destroyed it, I will rebuild Tartarus, and it will be much, much worse than this. The Olympians have little imagination when it comes to torture. And Hades will spend at least as long as I have in the darkness.'

Fury raged through me, my passion and my instinct to protect him too great to suppress.

'It's Zeus you're angry with, not Hades!' I could feel my power reacting, the image of Hades' face fueling my strength, as it always did. I couldn't let him live that life. I had to do something. And my vines agreed. With a ripple, they turned black.

'No!'

Cronos let out a long breath and closed his eyes as black tattoos began to spread across his shoulders.

'No!' I screamed again, desperately trying to disintegrate the vines. But it was as though they were glued to him, he was too strong. And then the power flowing down them from him hit me, and everything stopped.

Time itself stood still as power consumed me, so vast

I could make no sense of it. Within seconds it was over-whelming me, I was drowning in the infinite; swirling through a mass of light and shadow that never ended.

'Persephone!'

That voice... I knew that voice. That voice was the most important thing in the world to me. More important than anything else. I clung to it, the dizzying vortex around me slowing.

It was Hades.

As I came back to reality I saw Hades, hulking and furious, a canon of blue light beating uselessly at my vines. Legions of blue bodies were climbing up Cronos' expanding form, but Cronos wasn't reacting, his arms open wide, black vine tattoos spreading further across his body.

'Persephone, stop the vines! I can't flash you out while you're connected to him!' Hades roared, but I couldn't speak. Tidal waves of power were rolling through me, leaving me utterly breathless, images of worlds beyond my wildest imaginings flashing before me.

'Persy! Persy, tell me how to help you!'

Skop. I could hear Skop's voice.

'Worship me.' I was vaguely aware that the words were coming from my own lips, and Hades' eyes locked on mine, filled with dread as more blue light powered from him, into Cronos. 'Olympus will know true fear. True power. True death,' my voice thundered.

Stop! My mind railed against the words I was saying,

but the little voice in my head, the one that really belonged to me, was too small, too quiet, too weak. Cronos was taking over. His power was filling me, burning away everything else.

Pain, that had been indistinguishable from the torrent of emotion and power at first, was growing. Burning agony exploded suddenly in my head, and I cried out.

Desperation took over Hades' face, before blackness filled his silver eyes in a rush. The monster was taking over.

'You're too late, Hades!' said Cronos, his calm, soothing tone gone. 'I am becoming weak. Which means she has most of my power already.'

My head swam, a storm raging inside me.

'Never!' bellowed Hades, and raised his gleaming black trident. I could only just see them both, my eyes streaming as another pulse of agony ripped through me, the flood of images pouring through my mind blurring with reality. I could hardly breathe.

I started to fall to my knees as Hades brought his trident down on my vines with a roar.

I felt the reaction from Cronos before it occurred. The full wrath of Hades was enough to loosen his control. It was enough.

The second I felt the magnetic pull weaken, I willed the vines to disintegrate with everything I had. I tumbled forward as they disappeared, but instead of falling onto the rocky ground, I fell into Hades' arms and the world flashed white as Cronos screamed.

TWENTY-NINE

PERSEPHONE

I gasped for air as an awful sound reached my ears, my insides twisting and churning as white-hot pain burned through my veins.

'Persephone,' choked Hades, and I realized the sound was coming from him. I blinked up at his face, trying to force out the cascade of power ripping through me long enough to focus. I was lying in his arms, bare wasteland around us.

'Where are we?' I gulped.

'The surface,' he said, and I realized tears were streaming down his beautiful face.

'You need to take me somewhere I can't kill anyone,' I said, panic causing another swell of pain to grip me.

'Use your gold vines. Give me the power,' Hades said, gripping my jaw in his hand.

'Will-will it kill you?' I ground out, my head swimming again.

'No, it won't kill me,' he said, desperation in his eyes. I knew he was lying.

'It will fill you with darkness,' I whispered, knowing the truth of my words. He didn't respond.

Pouring Cronos' power into Hades would cause him to lose his soul as surely as if Cronos had broken free.

'My soul doesn't matter, as long as you live,' Hades breathed, pulling my face to his. Another wave of infinite power sent me into a spasm, and I could feel the pressure building inside me, tortuously painful. I couldn't contain it. I knew I couldn't. I was going to die. And I couldn't take Virgo or Hades with me.

'I love you,' I said, and an unexpected calm cut through the storm swirling inside my mind. 'I'm so glad I found you.' More tears rolled down Hades' face, his breath hot on my cheek as he kissed my face, over and over.

'Please, please, Persephone, give the power to me.' I pushed my numb hand into my pocket, and closed it around Poseidon's pearl, and lifted my other to Hades' wet cheek.

'Don't let the monster win. Ever. You're stronger than it is.'

'Persephone, I love you. Please, please. You can't leave me again.'

I pulled him to me, pressing my lips against his for the final time. Then I crushed the pearl in my hand.

.   .   .

Freezing ocean water cascaded over us and Hades cried out in surprise. I pulled myself to my feet, my vision blurry and my whole body numb as Buddy whinnied into existence beside me. And as I had hoped, he wasn't a seahorse. He was a *winged* horse.

'I love you. You have to let me do this,' I said, looking into Hades anguished face.

'I love you,' he choked, and I pulled myself awkwardly onto Buddy's back. He began to gallop immediately, then his huge wings snapped taut, and we launched into the sky. The waves of pain were increasing now, and I gripped his mane as tightly as I could as we soared higher.

'When I tell you, you've got to get out of here, Buddy,' I whispered to the horse, and he neighed loudly. Poseidon said he could be out of water for five minutes. And to make sure I killed nobody when the power overcame me, I needed to be as high as I could be, as far from everything and everyone in Olympus as possible.

We flew on, higher and higher, and when I could barely see Hades on the rock below, and the pressure inside me was so painful I knew I couldn't bare it any longer, I let go. I let go of Buddy, I let go of the power, I let go of myself. Completely.

A clarity I had never known descended over me as the horse vanished, and I hovered, weightless, suspended in time and space. I stared around myself, gaping, as the pain stopped immediately. A swirling mass of light and shadow was surrounding me, and with a jolt, I realized the power hadn't left me yet.

For the few moments before it overwhelmed me, at that suspended point in time, the power belonged to me. I had magic and strength unparalleled. And as it glowed and swirled around me, understanding came to me.

It wasn't all dark.

Daylight and shadow, light and dark; they both swirled together.

Hades' words sang through my mind. 'You can't keep a light that bright in the dark.' But what other purpose did a bright light serve, if it wasn't lighting the dark? One could not exist without the other. One had no purpose without the other. Light was destined to live with the dark.

I knew what I had to do. I knew it with bone deep certainty. I needed to light the dark.

My vines burst from my palms, gleaming gold, and as I began to fall through the air, I shot them at the surface of Virgo. They slammed into the ground, and I heard Hades shout over the rushing wind, as I drew every bit of light I could from Cronos' power and channeled it into the rock. Life flared bright inside me, rushing through my body, and I focused on Hades' face, on love and light and growth.

And I felt the dark around me, inside me, changing. The shadows in the swirling mass were receding, the light forcing them out. The torrents of power that had been battering against me now flowed through me and into my golden vines like a river of life, and as I approached the surface, green invaded my blurred vision.

Too late I realized I was going to hit the ground, and with my vines connected to the earth I couldn't use them to brace myself. But instead of hard rock, I hit something soft. I was on a cushion of blue light, and as it lowered me gently to the floor, Hades ran toward me.

His face was a mask of awe and shock, and as I channeled the last of the glittering power into the ground, I called out to him.

'A light this bright was made for the dark. They belong together.' My vines disintegrated as he reached me, and he barely slowed, scooping me off my feet and kissing me so hard I couldn't breathe.

'You're alive,' he said, over and over between kisses. Exhilaration rocketed through me, and as the remnants of the godly power left me, my own emotions finally took hold of me again. *I was alive. And so was he.*

'We both are,' I gasped, and kissed him back, just as hard.

Eventually he set me back down on my feet, staring into my eyes like he'd never seen anything so mesmerizing.

I'd done it. I had actually saved us. I had channeled that immense power into something good, and light. I hadn't let it overwhelm me. I had been strong enough to save us. Disbelief was making me giddy as I stared up at Hades. If I had truly filled his realm with light, then there was a chance for us. A real chance.

'I love you. I love you so much. Look what you've done to this place,' he said, gripping my shoulders and turning me around slowly.

We were standing in a glade, willow trees waving softly in a gentle breeze. Birds tweeted somewhere in the distance, and butterflies flitted between meadow flowers dotting the lush grass.

'Is the whole surface like this?' I asked, breathless. I wasn't sure how much I'd done.

Hades pulled my back close against his chest, wrapping his huge arms around me, and flashed. We hovered, high above the surface, where I'd been with Buddy just moments before. There wasn't a dusty, barren bit of rock anywhere. Streams meandered across the landscape, trees of every type and stature, flowers of every color and species filling the space. I could see a huge forest in the distance, and beyond that a green-covered valley, waterfalls cascading down one side.

Hades flashed again, and we were back in the glade. I spun in his arms, looking up into his eyes.

'This is still part of Virgo, so can you live here?' Hades raised his eyebrows at me, then closed his eyes. I felt his power rolling over me.

'We are far from the dark, where my power is most needed, but... you are right, this is still Virgo. It is still my realm.' Excitement lit up his stunning eyes as he opened them, and hope made my chest swell to the point it ached. 'Yes. Yes, I think I can.'

'We can live up here half of the time! We will get respite from the darkness, but you will still be in control of the Underworld!' Elation made my words fast, my voice high-pitched. *We could be together. We would be safe, together, light and dark as one.*

He pushed his hand into my hair, stroking his thumb down my jaw.

'Persephone, you... You complete me. You make me strong. You make me whole. You saved us.' Happiness gripped me, and I felt a lump in my throat as I stared back at him. 'I love you,' he said, his voice the softest, most sensual thing I'd ever heard.

'In that case,' I whispered, letting the happy tears come as I stood on tiptoes to kiss him, 'it's a damned good thing that I'm your new Queen.'

THIRTY

PERSEPHONE

As I realized what my words meant though, panic swelled through me. The Trial... Morpheus!

'Sam and Hecate! Hedone has them hostage! We have to stop Morpheus!'

We may have survived, and Cronos may still be trapped in Tartarus, but this wasn't over yet. Guilt swamped me as the emotion and power crashing through my brain started to clear, and the full impact of everything I'd learned in the last hour began to filter through. *The volcano. Zeus. My brother and Hecate.*

Hades' face darkened, and the world flashed around us.

I gaped at the scene before me in the judgment hall, my power-addled body and brain simply not keeping up.

'Persy!' My brother charged toward me, lifting me off

my feet as he reached me. 'Thank god you're OK.' I squeezed him back as I stared over his shoulder.

Tied up with chains made from some sort of glowing metal, were Morpheus and Hedone, and they were both sitting on Minthe's red chariot. Kerato and two other guards had spears pointed at them and Morpheus bared his teeth at me.

Minthe and Sanape were standing nearby, and were both covered in blood. The spirit who had been driving their chariot appeared to be tending their wounds.

'What happened?' I breathed, as Sam let me go. 'Where's Hecate?'

'I'm here,' she said from behind us, and I whirled, relieved to see that she looked fine as she strode forward. 'I'm sorry, boss. She knocked me out.' Her eyes dipped to the floor as she reached Hades.

'They managed to manacle me, so I'd be a hypocrite to reprimand you,' Hades said, an edge of steel to his tone.

'They manacled you?' Hecate gasped. 'Zeus is a fucking asshole, I swear if he ever-'

'Who detained Morpheus?' Hades said, cutting her off.

'Minthe,' answered my brother. 'It was pretty amazing actually.'

'Yeah, we owe her,' said Hecate. 'Ask her yourself, we were both out of it, so she can tell you best.'

'Minthe?' called Hades, and the mountain nymph

looked over at us, wincing. I glanced quickly at Hades, then hurried over to her, my gold vines snaking from my palms before I reached her.

'Let me help you,' I said, expecting an argument. But she just raised her wrist for my vine to coil round. 'Did you really save my brother?' I asked her as Hades stepped up behind me.

'That slutty bitch Hedone thought I was too injured to be a threat. That'll teach her not to underestimate me,' Minthe snapped as my healing power began to flow into her. She closed her eyes, a look of relief washing over her face. Her tone was less angry when she spoke again. 'I was laid on the floor by the chariot, my arm and knee fucked, when I saw the portal and you and Morpheus through it. I heard everything. So I asked Poly,' she gestured at the spirit woman, 'to get help. Then Sanape and I jumped Hedone as soon as the portal was closed. Morpheus turned up not long after, but Sanape is a seriously good shot.' Sanape gave me a vicious grin and I glanced over my shoulder at Morpheus, restrained in the chariot. Silver liquid was dribbling from his temple. 'Kerato and the guards got here with the chains just in time, I'm not sure we could have held them much longer.'

'Thank you,' I breathed, and threw my arms around her before I could stop myself. She stiffened in my embrace, and then muttered,

'You can stop the healing now, I'm good. Help Sanape.' I let her go, and did as she asked, the Amazon woman looking reluctant to receive my help, but accepting when Minthe gave her a long enough look.

'Minthe, the Underworld owes you a debt,' said Hades. She looked at him, then bowed her head.

'I owed Persephone a debt. It's now clear.' She had a hard glint in her eye when she looked back at me.

'Yes, yes of course it is,' I said.

'I can't bestow immortality on you, as you know it is forbidden for any single god to do that. But I can make you rich. You will have diamonds to last you a lifetime,' Hades said.

Minthe's mouth opened slowly, her eyebrows raising.

'Thank you, King Hades,' she breathed, dipping her head again.

'You too, Sanape,' he said, turning to the Amazon. She dipped her head less reverently, but pride was stamped across her expression.

Hades turned, and strode to the chariot. I released the vines that had now healed Sanape, and followed him, nerves skittering through my stomach. Hedone was asleep, looking peaceful as she sat back-to-back with Morpheus.

'You can only save her from her punishment for so long,' Hades said, and his voice was like ice.

'I'll keep her asleep as long as I can,' answered Morpheus, not looking up. 'This is not her fault. She wanted to hurt nobody.'

'Unlike you?'

'I am fighting for a higher cause. I am fighting for Olympus. Cronos said there would be casualties.'

Blue light flared around Hades, and all the color drained from Morpheus' face abruptly. He seemed to shrink in on himself, and I saw gooseflesh raise on his skin. A small whimper escaped his mouth.

'You are as bound to your role as the dream god as I am to mine,' hissed Hades, 'and only that will save you from Tartarus. But you will perform that role as a prisoner to your own fear, for the rest of your immortal life, Morpheus. What you see in your mind now, is what you will see every minute of every day and night.'

'No,' he whispered, finally lifting his haunted eyes to Hades. 'No, please!'

'Take him to his rooms, and bind him,' Hades said, and Hecate stepped forward.

'With pleasure, boss,' she said, and with a flash, they both disappeared. Hedone fell backward without him to lean on, and moaned softly.

'Kerato, confine her in the palace until Aphrodite can deal with her, as she is one of her deities.'

'Yes, my Lord,' the minotaur said.

'What did you make Morpheus see?' I asked Hades quietly, as the minotaur pulled Hedone groggily to her feet, and the chariot lifted off the temple floor.

'It doesn't matter,' he answered.

But it did. The punishment was hitting me hard. Because I had an awful feeling I was going to live the same life. I was going to see all those people I had killed

over and over again, every day. Those screaming, inno-
cent people, running hopelessly from the lava.

My thoughts were either clear on my face or made it
through the bond, because Hades pulled me to him,
tipping my face up to his.

'Cronos did that, not you. You were a conduit, a
vessel, a weapon. Not the cause. Do you understand?' I
nodded, trying to believe his words. 'And you are no
longer that person. Look at what you did up there. You
controlled the power this time, and saved the lives of
thousands. Possibly more.'

This time, his words did hit home. Saved the life of
thousands. He was right. New Persephone saved lives.

I would never forgive myself for what I knew I had
done, but at least I was making a start on setting it right.

A bright flash was followed quickly by the smell of the
ocean, and then Poseidon was stood before us, Dionysus
at his side.

'Skop!' The gnome sitting on Dionysus' shoulder shifted
into a dog as he jumped down and ran to me. I crouched and
pulled the dog into a hug. 'I'm so glad you're OK.'

'And boy am I glad to see you too,' he said.

'Zeus escaped,' said Poseidon, and I stood up fast, my
attention on the sea god. 'He severely wounded Ares and
Artemis, and Hera has withdrawn completely, and won't
talk to anyone.'

'Shit,' hissed Hades.

'Shit doesn't cover half of it,' said Dionysus. 'He's got that fire Titan of yours with him, she came and busted him out of Ares' hold.'

'But he hates Titans!' I exclaimed.

'If Ankhiale knew that Cronos wasn't going to be free, she will move to the next strongest god,' Hades muttered. 'And Zeus won't turn down allies now.'

'So, does that mean you're at war?' I asked slowly.

'No. Zeus hasn't declared any such thing, but he will need to face a trial and punishment. Just like Hades did, when he broke the rules,' Poseidon said with a pointed look at Hades.

'Is that why he has run?'

'Yes. He'll be back, I've no doubt. With an elaborate excuse for all of this, and a new plan to inflate his ego further.'

'He is a dangerous maniac, and he can no longer rule the Olympians,' said Hades. Dionysus nodded.

'Hear, hear. The man needs to chill the fuck out.'

'We will deal with succession later. For now, I'm here to see Persephone,' said Poseidon. I gulped as the Lord of the Oceans turned to me. 'Your handling of Cronos' power bears the marks of a true Queen and goddess of Olympus. I am pleased to welcome you to our ranks.' My mouth fell open. 'And thank you for taking care of my hippocampus,' he added, before giving me a twinkling smile, and vanishing.

'Well done, Persy,' said Dionysus, as I blinked after Poseidon. 'Make sure you visit soon, there are some folk on Taurus who remember growing up with you now,' he said, with a big grin. 'And your fella needs a drink. I got lots of that.'

'I-I will,' I stuttered, and felt a smile take over my face. My future in Olympus was looking a whole lot better than I could have possibly imagined.

THIRTY-ONE

PERSEPHONE

I took a deep breath as I stared at my reflection in the grand mirror. Happiness so intense it made me want to scream washed through me. I was wearing an actual wedding dress.

I twirled, letting the white lace spin around the satin slip beneath. The dress had been made for the occasion, and the top was a classic white corset, but the bottom... The bottom was miles upon miles of white lace that I had designed myself. An intricate pattern of roses and skulls. Earth and nature, dark and light, life and death.

It had been a month since Cronos had almost killed me and I'd used his power to turn the surface of Virgo into a nature-filled haven for the two of us. Hades used his power to build us a modest hut, to see if we really could live above the ground. He had been nervous at first that the longer he was above the surface of Virgo, the less control he would have over his realm and the dangerous demons he was linked to. Mostly, he feared losing his grip on Tartarus.

But it was a full two weeks before he felt any difference in his power, and so for the following two weeks, we returned to his rooms in the palace, below the surface. His control strengthened again immediately.

I saw no reason we couldn't live like that for eternity, spending half our time in the light, and half in the dark. Especially since I had some pretty epic plans for the house in the glade.

I looked down at the ring on my finger, a thrill of anticipation whipping through my body. *Married*. I was actually getting married.

It hadn't taken much to convince Hades to do the 'human' down-on-one-knee proposal. In fact, I'd just asked Hecate to tell him that was what he was supposed to do. And he went one step further. The culture in Olympus was to have one ring, for both the engagement and wedding, but because he knew that there were usually two rings in my world, he'd made a special ring for me. It was a silver band, tiny swirling vines engraved on it, and it had a section cut out all the way through, where a second tiny gold ring fitted, the ends meeting in little Greek spirals. It was the most precious thing I'd ever owned.

'Are you ready?'

I grinned as I turned, and Hecate beamed back at me. She was wearing a blue dress, and it was the first time I'd ever seen her wear something floor length. Like me, she had white roses weaved into her hair.

'As I'll ever be.'

'Here,' she said, and passed me a saucer of fizzy wine. 'A toast. To the new Queen of the Underworld.' A stupid smile stretched my cheeks as I clinked my glass with hers and sipped. The freaking Queen of the Underworld.

'I'm really, really not happy about this,' came Skop's voice, and he waddled into the room, Sam striding beside him.

'You look great,' I told him, and he scowled at me from under his beard.

'I'd rather be a dog than wear clothes. This is the most unnatural thing I've ever done,' he answered, pulling at the ill-fitting pants he had on. I laughed.

'You can be a dog if you like, but it'll make drinking and dancing a little hard. And before you ask for the millionth time, no, you can't be naked at my wedding.'

He gave a big, over-the-top sigh.

'If it was anyone else, I'd refuse,' he grumbled, rolling his eyes.

'Thank you Skop. You're the best,' I beamed at him.

'Don't you forget it. Best personal guard ever. Saved your damned life and you won't even let me be naked,' he muttered.

'You look amazing,' said my brother, leaning forward to kiss my cheek and saving me from having to respond to the kobaloi.

'Thank you. It's a shame mom and dad can't be here,' I said.

'Definitely for the best that they're not,' he grinned at me. 'And anyway, now you're all immortal and powerful and stuff, you can visit them next week.'

'Yes. I want Hades to meet them. But I'm not sure who or what to tell them he is. Maybe a lawyer?' Sam snorted.

'Right. A terrifying, football-playing, body-building lawyer.'

'We've got to go, Persy,' said Hecate, cutting across our conversation. 'This is not something you want to be late for.' More excited nerves rippled through me and she smiled as she reached for my hand.

I linked my arm through my brother's as the doors to the breakfast room opened, and the harps began to play. The blossom tree was in full bloom, and light streamed through the huge arched windows, gold frames sparkling and lush green beyond. But my eyes were locked in place on the reason I was there.

Standing next to our tree, at the end of the aisle, was Hades. He was wearing a black toga lined with silver and the sight of him took my breath away. His eyes found mine as I stepped into the room, and as I saw delight wash over his beautiful face, his voice sounded in my head.

'You look... unbelievable.'

'So do you.'

'I can't believe you're marrying me. Again. I'm the luckiest man in the world.'

I beamed at him as I walked down the aisle toward him. He was my everything. 'I love you.'

'And I love you, my Queen.'

THE END

READ ON FOR A SNEAK PREVIEW OF WHAT HAPPENS NEXT, IN THE GOD OF WAR'S STORY...

"**B**ella, please, put me down." I barely heard the words over the blood pounding in my ears. But I knew the voice…

"Bella, I'd really, really appreciate it if you could just let go of my neck."

The red mist was making my vision cloudy, obscuring the man in front of me, who was pinned to the wall by my hand across his throat.

But I knew his voice…

"Bella, please." The voice was scratchy and choked but…

"Joshua!" I cried, dropping my rigid arm immediately, the fury raging through my body dissipating as guilt swamped me. "Shit, shit, shit, I did it again, didn't I?"

Joshua slid down the magnolia-painted wall opposite me, clutching at his throat, his eyes red.

"Yeah. Yeah, you did."

"Why? Why am I like this?" I couldn't keep the bitterness from my voice as I crouched to him, pulling him to his feet.

"That's what therapy is going to help you with, Bella," he said, blinking slowly and twisting his neck as we walked back toward to his desk, and the long couch I always sat on.

"But I've been seeing you for months, and I'm no better." Anger started to rekindle in my gut, the frustration of not being able to control myself a delicious fuel for my rage. Nothing set off the rage like frustration.

"Anger management therapy is a long process. You're doing great," Joshua said, and sat down in his chair.

I slumped down on the patient couch and cocked my head at him. My skin was still fizzing from the adrenaline that always accompanied an episode.

"How many times will you let me attack you before you quit on me?" I whispered. I didn't actually want to know the answer. I just couldn't face watching the only man who had ever tried to help me, suffer at my own hands over and over again.

"I'm tougher than I look, Bella. I'm not going anywhere."

He smiled at me, most of the strain on his face now gone, and I so badly wanted to believe him.

I knew it was wrong to have be in love with your your shrink. But, in my defense, he was freaking hot. Dark hair flopped over his forehead and curled around his ears, and his hazel eyes were permanently calm and soothing, a balm to my own constant million-mile-an-hour energy.

And he looked tough enough to me. My eyes flicked over his body.

Broad shoulders.

Rounded biceps.

Big red mark on his neck... I'd done that. I'd *just* done that. Guilt made me feel sick, twisting my stomach in knots. Joshua was the only person who had ever truly tried to help me.

But when the red mist descended, I was no longer Bella; mostly decent, if a little hyper, human being. I was a freaking nutjob. And strong to boot. It was as though anger made me physically more powerful, and danger-ous. Rational thought abandoned me, my normal senses overtaken by the red mist.

And the worst part was, I desired it. When I was younger, I hadn't tried to fight it. The feeling of strength and control was like a drug, and I allowed the craving for confrontation to run wild. Every fight I won, I revelled, no matter if the person I kicked the shit out of deserved it or not. Every time someone underestimated me, at five foot two with my pixie-face and blonde hair, I took plea-sure in smashing their preconceptions to bits. And it wasn't just their preconceptions I smashed. I smashed *everything*.

When I got too old for the cops to keep letting me out, I got more careful. But I didn't stop.

When I was busted for fighting in the gambling rings, they gave me a six month sentence. When I fought with every cellmate I had, I was put in solitary confinement.

And then I got sad. Like really, really sad. Being

completely alone sucked. But in the absence of anyone to pick a fight with, I could think clearly for the first time in my life. I realized I needed to control my anger, and I needed to vent it on the right people. The people who deserved their asses booted into next week.

"Tell me again about the dream," Joshua said.

"But what if it triggers me again?"

"We need to find out what causes the episodes. I accept the risk that comes with that," he replied, gently.

I shook my head.

"No. No, I don't think we should carry on. I've already hurt you once today."

"You're not a bad person, Bella. The anger in you is chemical, it's not part of your soul. Remember that."

I said nothing. Because he was wrong. My issue wasn't a chemical imbalance. It was more than that. I'd known something was wrong with me my whole life.

Joshua sighed. "Will you join us for the group session today?"

I nodded. I hated group therapy. Everyone there pissed me off. But Joshua insisted it was good for me, and I felt bad about what I'd done to his neck.

"Sure," I said.

"Good. Are you sure you don't want to carry on now?"

"I'm sure," I told him. "I'll go for a quick run round the block, burn off some energy 'til group starts."

"Good idea," he smiled. "See you in twenty minutes."

. . .

"You're a decent human, you're a decent human," I chanted to myself as I jogged down Fleet Street, avoiding tourists and biting back impatient comments. Holy jalapeno, but these morons moved slowly.

Maybe I should move. London was filled to the brim with angry energy. It couldn't be helping me calm down.

But I couldn't leave London. Not because I had family here or anything. Hell, I didn't even have any friends, let alone family. I couldn't leave London because of the theaters.

Since I'd moved to London from New Jersey ten years ago, I'd saved every spare bit of cash I could scrabble together from the menial, shitty jobs I could never hold onto, to spend on the theater. I didn't have the patience for books, and I could barely sit still through an entire movie, but there was something completely mesmerizing about the theater to me. I attributed every moral fiber in my being to what I had learned through plays and musicals. Empathy seemed to pour into me from nowhere when I watched the fictional stories play out so vividly before me, the actors giving it everything they had and every second sucking me in further.

No, I couldn't leave London. Even though since losing my last shitty job I couldn't afford the theater any more. But at least I'd learned a valuable lesson; I did not have the right temperament to be a bartender in a city. Drunk assholes were a big fucking trigger for my temper. I sucked in air as I jogged faster.

I'd find another job. Soon. I had to, or me and my stuck-up cat would end up hungry and homeless.

"You're a decent human," I repeated through clenched teeth, flipping my middle finger at a cyclist who was swerving around me on the wrong side of the road.

When I got back to Joshua's building I headed straight for the washroom and changed my t-shirt. I let my hair out of its bun and tried to make it look somewhat attractive, then gave up, glaring at my reflection instead.

Why the hell would a man who I regularly attacked and knew how much of a freak I was, be attracted to me?

I blew out a sigh. At least he *knew* I was a freak. Unlike all the other poor bastards I'd dated. The first they'd known of it was when something innocuous triggered the mist and I went freaking crazy on their ass. Me and dating did not go well together.

But Joshua... There was something in his eyes when he looked at me, I was sure of it. Something deeper than just professional patience. He cared about me.

"Yeah, keep telling yourself that, freakface," I muttered at my reflection. But that was fear talking. Fear manifesting as shit-talking and aggression. He had taught me that, in our sessions.

I was scared he would turn me down, and then I wouldn't be able to face him again. I would lose him, and his help.

But imagine how much better my life would be if he did like me. Imagine having someone to share each day, and night, with. Imagine him kissing me...

I stood straighter as I made my decision. I was going to tell him how I felt.

If he wasn't interested then he wouldn't be a dick about it, that wasn't his way. I would just go home with a red face, eat my bodyweight in ice cream and then spend a few hours with my punch-bag. Maybe avoid him for a week.

But if he said yes... Those soft eyes, that gentle voice, those expressive hands.

The best-case scenario outweighed the worst-case.

I was early, so there was nobody else around as I pushed the double doors to the lecture room open. My heart hammered in my chest as I stepped into the room. I was really going to do this. I was going to tell him how I felt. Maybe not that I was in love with him, I didn't want to scare the shit out of him.

Joshua was a part-time university psychology lecturer, part-time anger management shrink. The university let him use his office for one-on-one sessions, and a lecture room for group. I'd never made it to university. Surprise, surprise.

Sadly Joshua's building wasn't one of the many beautiful old university structures that dotted London and looked like something out of a fairytale. It was a concrete monstrosity built in the seventies, and the lecture room looked like any other boring office, just a bit larger, with lots of cheap plastic chairs.

I stumbled as I reached the ring of seats set out for us

crazies in the middle of the room. Someone was lying on the floor, in the center of the chairs.

Joshua.

"Joshua?" I ran forward, dropping to my knees beside him, about to turn him onto his back when I froze. Blood. There was blood, pooling beneath him, reaching my knees. But if the blood was spreading now, this must have just happened.

I leaped to my feet, my fists raised, my muscles swelling.

"Where are you?" I roared at the unknown threat. "Show yourself!"

The air in front of me shimmered, and then there was a blinding white flash. My hands moved to cover my eyes instinctively, and I could feel the anger building inside me.

I was ready to fight.

I dropped my arms and blinked rapidly, clearing my eyes.

And gaped.

A man was standing the other side of Joshua. And he looked like no man I'd ever seen.

He was seven feet tall at least, and was wearing gleaming golden armor like a freaking Roman soldier. His face was covered by a massive shining helmet with a red plume, and his arms and legs were made of muscles, thick ropes of it wrapping around his limbs like Arnold fucking Schwarzenegger.

He reached out with his sandaled foot and poked at Joshua.

"What the fuck are you doing?" I yelled, darting toward him. "Why have you done this?"

The eyes in the helmet snapped to mine.

"You are more interested in challenging me than saving him? That confirms it. You are the right one," the man said, his voice deep and abrupt. His words took me aback, and I realized he was right. I needed to help Joshua.

I shoved my hand in my back pocket, pulling out my cellphone and fumbling to unlock it.

"Stay right there! I don't know why you've done this, but I'm calling the police!"

The man ignored me, flipping Joshua over with his foot, and there was an awful squelching noise. Blood soaked the front of his shirt.

"Is he dead?" Please, please, please don't let him be dead, I prayed, the backs of my eyes burning.

"Yes. He is dead."

I felt a wave of dizziness wash over me, my stomach flipping.

"No, no he can't be." I dropped to my knees again, feeling for a pulse in his neck.

There was nothing.

"His human body is dead. The police will think you did this," said the man simply.

"What?"

"You are here, alone with the body. And human police are fools."

"*Human* police? Who the fuck are you?"

I glared up at the armored giant, my head swimming, red seeping into my vision. This couldn't be happening.

"I am Ares, God of War."

"Ares? The fucking Greek god?"

"Yes. Stop saying fuck. It is unladylike."

"Unladylike?" I realized I was yelling as I got unsteadily to my feet. "Why did you kill him?"

"Stupid girl. I did not kill him. And only his human body is dead. His immortal body has been kidnapped, taken to Olympus."

I felt myself sway slightly, then a surge of adrenaline shot through my veins, steadying me.

"You need to start talking sense right fucking now," I hissed.

The huge man glared at me a few seconds, then sighed.

"I am Ares, the God of War. And you are Enyo, Goddess of War. I am here to kill you."

Pre-order The Warrior God here.

THANKS FOR READING!

Thank you so much for reading this take on Hades and Persephone's story.

I've been obsessed with Greek mythology for as long as I can remember, and I can't tell you how much I love sitting down every day to bring characters from that rich world of craziness to life. The moral message, the mutual sacrifice, the intense love between Hades and Persephone, that perfect balance of two such different beings, has always been right up there with my favorites of all the myths, and I have LOVED writing this story.

'Love conquers all' is the theme behind everything I write, and that comes in no small part from the love I get from my own husband. He's my biggest fan, despite having never read anything I've written (he's not a reader - I'll get him to listen to the audiobooks one day). But he listens to me and supports me and helps me in all the other ways I need it and I am eternally grateful.

I am also in awe of how much help and support complete strangers have given me during my journey as a writer. Reena, I can't believe you actually sent me the ring, from Greece, that inspired Persephone's wedding ring!! (Picture on next page!) You make my books better and I'm so thankful for your help and support and friendship! Brittany, thank you for your sharp eye and experienced early opinions! Mum, thanks for proofreading everything I write, even if it's a bit steamy. And for trying to keep the naughty books away from Grandad…

I will keep writing about all the incredible gods from the ancient Greek world until I run out, and I'm pretty sure that won't happen. Next up is Ares, and I am very, very excited about it.

Hecate turned out way more fun than I had originally expected, so I have a follow on novel for her planned too.

Thank you again, fabulous reader, for making it possible for me to keep writing!!

Eliza xxx

**The ring Reena sent me from Greece -
Persephone's wedding ring!!**

You can get exclusive first looks at artwork and story ideas, plus free short stories and audiobooks if you sign up to my newsletter at elizaraine.com and you can hang out with me and get teasers, giveaways and release updates (and pictures of my pets) by joining my Facebook reader group here!

Printed in Great Britain
by Amazon

60129057R00151